FRAILS CAN BE SO TOUGH

by

HANK JANSON

This edition first published in England in 2004
by Telos Publishing Ltd
61 Elgar Avenue, Tolworth, Surrey, KT5 9JP, England

www.telos.co.uk
Telos Publishing Ltd values feedback.
Please e-mail us with any comments you may have
about this book to: feedback@telos.co.uk

ISBN: 1-903889-88-X

Novel by Stephen D Frances
Cover by Reginald Heade
With thanks to Steve Holland
www.hankjanson.co.uk
Silhouette device by Philip Mendoza
Cover design by David J Howe
This edition prepared for publication by Stephen James Walker
Internal design, typesetting and layout by David Brunt

First published in England by New Fiction Press, August 1951

Printed in India

1 2 3 4 5 6 7 8 9 10 11 12 13 14 15

British Library Cataloguing in Publication Data. A catalogue
record for this book is available from the British Library.

FRAILS CAN BE SO TOUGH

THE CLASSIC HANK JANSON

The first original Hank Janson book appeared in 1946, and the last in 1971. However, the classic era on which we are focusing in the Telos reissue series lasted from 1946 to 1953.

The following is a checklist of those books, which were subdivided into five main series and a number of "specials".

The titles so far reissued by Telos are indicated by way of an asterisk.

Pre-series books

When Dames Get Tough (1946) *
Scarred Faces (1946) *

Series One

1 This Woman Is Death (1948)
2 Lady, Mind That Corpse (1948)
3 Gun Moll For Hire (1948)
4 No Regrets For Clara (1949)
5 Smart Girls Don't Talk (1949)
6 Lilies For My Lovely (1949)
7 Blonde On The Spot (1949)
8 Honey, Take My Gun (1949)
9 Sweetheart, Here's Your Grave (1949)
10 Gunsmoke In Her Eyes (1949)
11 Angel, Shoot To Kill (1949)
12 Slay-Ride For Cutie (1949)

Series Two

13 Sister, Don't Hate Me (1949)
14 Some Look Better Dead (1950) *
15 Sweetie, Hold Me Tight (1950)
16 Torment For Trixie (1950)
17 Don't Dare Me, Sugar (1950)
18 The Lady Has A Scar (1950)
19 The Jane With The Green Eyes (1950)
20 Lola Brought Her Wreath (1950)
21 Lady, Toll The Bell (1950)
22 The Bride Wore Weeds (1950)
23 Don't Mourn Me Toots (1951)
24 This Dame Dies Soon (1951)

Series Three

25 Baby, Don't Dare Squeal (1951)
26 Death Wore A Petticoat (1951)
27 Hotsy, You'll Be Chilled (1951)
28 It's Always Eve That Weeps (1951)
29 Frails Can Be So Tough (1951) *
30 Milady Took The Rap (1951)
31 Women Hate Till Death (1951) *
32 Broads Don't Scare Easy (1951)
33 Skirts Bring Me Sorrow (1951) *
34 Sadie Don't Cry Now (1952)
35 The Filly Wore A Rod (1952)
36 Kill Her If You Can (1952)

Series Four

37 Murder (1952)
38 Conflict (1952)
39 Tension (1952)
40 Whiplash (1952)
41 Accused (1952) *
42 Killer (1952) *
43 Suspense (1952)
44 Pursuit (1953)
45 Vengeance (1953)
46 Torment (1953) *
47 Amok (1953)
48 Corruption (1953)

Series Five

49 Silken Menace (1953)
50 Nyloned Avenger (1953)

Specials

A Auctioned (1952)
B Persian Pride (1952)
C Desert Fury (1953)
D Unseen Assassin (1953)
E One Man In His Time (1953)
F Deadly Mission (1953)

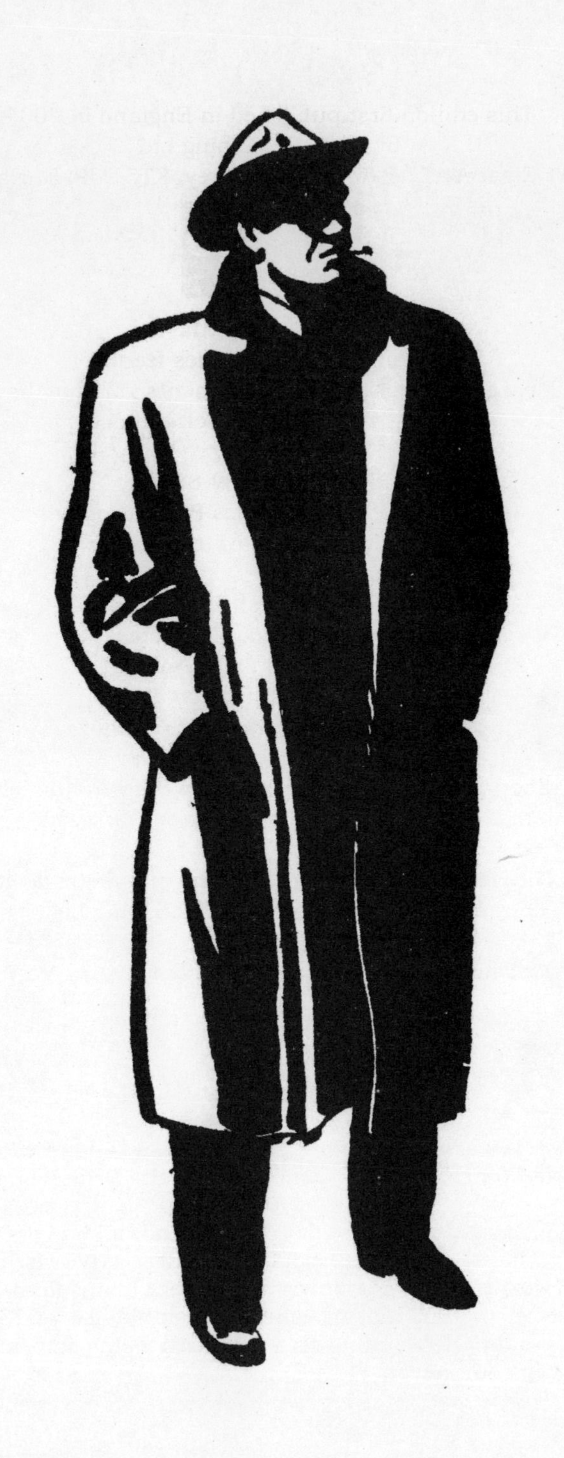

PUBLISHER'S NOTE

The appeal of the Hank Janson books to a modern readership lies not only in the quality of the storytelling, which is as powerfully compelling today as it was when they were first published, but also in the fascinating insight they afford into the attitudes, customs and morals of the 1940s and 1950s. We have therefore endeavoured to make *Frails Can Be So Tough*, and all our other Hank Janson reissues, as faithful to the original editions as possible. Unlike some other publishers, who when reissuing vintage fiction have been known edit it to remove aspects that might offend present-day sensibilities, we have left the original narrative absolutely intact.

The original editions of these classic Hank Janson titles made quite frequent use of phonetic "Americanisms" such as "kinda", "gotta", "wanna" and so on. Again, we have left these unchanged in the Telos Publishing Ltd reissues, to give readers as genuine as possible a taste of what it was like to read these books when they first came out, even though such devices have since become sorta out of fashion.

The only way in which we have amended the original text has been to correct obvious lapses in spelling, grammar and punctuation – we have, for instance, added question marks in the not-infrequent cases where they were omitted from the ends of questions in the original – and to remedy clear typesetting errors.

Lastly, we should mention that we have made every effort to trace and acquire relevant copyrights in the various elements that make up this book. However, if anyone has any further information that they could provide in this regard, we would be very grateful to receive it.

INTRODUCTION

Frails Can Be So Tough, the twenty-ninth novel to carry the Hank Janson byline, was published in August 1951, when the business of producing Hank Janson novels was in a period of transition.

Hank's creator, Stephen D Frances, was making plans to move abroad, having become enchanted by an isolated village on the Costa Brava that he had discovered whilst holidaying in Spain some years earlier. Rosas (Rhodaes as it was originally known) had been founded by Greek settlers who entered Spain in 630 BC and settled along the east coast; Frances, following the road down towards Barcelona over 2,500 years later, had discovered the village by accident. Nestled under the mountain foothills of northern Spain, some fifty kilometres from the French border, it had captivated Frances with its rugged, volcanic coastline that looked out over bays and coves and a wide expanse of unspoiled beach. "Its savage beauty was breathtaking," he later recalled. He had driven into Rosas in search of food, but stayed for weeks. Some of the locals he met during that first visit became lifelong friends.

Back in Britain, Frances had a business to run. As well as writing the Hank Janson novels, he also had to chase down paper supplies, organize the printing and reprinting of novels and arrange deliveries of the finished books. Their success was staggering in the post-war climate of rationing and paper control, and Frances had high hopes that he would be able to retire from the time-consuming, daily grind of publishing and confine himself to writing. In 1949, he had met Reginald Herbert Carter, a sales rep for The Racecourse Press, who had begun printing Hank Janson novels on their rotary presses soon after, pushing the print runs and profits up even further until Frances's one-man operation had a turnover greater than many small businesses that employed two or three hundred workers.

By early 1951, Frances had been able to give up freelance writing for other companies and was concentrating solely on Hank and, at Carter's suggestion, was looking into the possibilities of buying up a bankrupt company with a large trading loss to produce the Janson novels, putting the publishing side of the Hank Janson operation on a more formal business footing as well as benefiting from a quite considerable tax break. Carter also knew where he could buy a rotary press, and was in the process of setting up Arc Press with distributor Julius Reiter. This would vertically integrate the whole operation from writing to distribution and allow Frances, Carter and Reiter to enjoy the profits that Hank Janson generated at each step.

Once the idea was in place, Frances took the decision to move to Spain permanently, hoping to live an idyllic life overlooking the bay at Rosas, making a substantial living writing new Hank Janson adventures.

In August 1951, Carter took over Editions Poetry (London) Ltd., and bought the rights to Hank from Frances for a princely £4,000 (worth about £75,000 nowadays). The figure was nonsensically low against the value of books and debts – about £30,000-worth (around £500,000 in today's currency) – that Frances also passed on, having accumulated this in just two and a half years.

Frails Can Be So Tough was the first title to be issued by Carter under the New Fiction Press imprint. It was also the first to suffer the indignity of having its intended Reginald Heade cover artwork censored prior to publication, in an attempt by Carter to forestall possible prosecutions for obscenity. In its place appeared a sedate red and yellow silhouette against a plain green background.

The original intended artwork of a green-eyed blonde with a riding crop is reinstated for the first time on the cover of this Telos Publishing Ltd reissue, although some collectors may have a sneaking suspicion that they've seen the girl somewhere before. If you're lucky enough to have a copy of the earlier Hank Janson novel *Honey, Take My Gun*, you will recognise the same green-eyed blonde *. Presumably Heade used the same model on both occasions.

Despite the lack of Heade's striking cover, *Frails* still sold well on first publication: a second edition, primarily red with an orange "TV screen" title panel and green lettering, appeared only four or five months later. With the print runs of new Janson novels running to fifty or sixty thousand copies, we

---

* Heade's cover illustration for *Honey, Take My Gun* was also used on the American Checkerbook reprint of another Hank Janson novel, *Lady, Mind That Corpse*.

can estimate that sales of new titles around that time were between ten and fifteen thousand a month.

Frails Can Be So Tough is a typical, solid example of a Hank Janson novel that demonstrates why his fans came back book after book. The third series of novels (they were broken down into groups of twelve) had begun with a run of stories without Hank Janson, the character, as their star. In most cases, this allowed Frances to tell far bleaker stories. They were still recounted in the first person, but by characters with dark pasts and deprived of Hank's moral code. Readers could experience the moral and physical struggles of the narrator even more intimately than when newspaperman Hank himself was the witness and recorder of events.

The basic plot of *Frails* was one that Frances had used previously, but with a twist. In previous books, the narrator was often a man wrongly accused of some crime who now seeks his revenge on the criminals (or, often, the so-called justice system) that put him in jail. In *Frails*, the narrator, Lee Shelton, has a far more personal reason for plotting retribution against nightclub owner J J Frisk, and a far more terrifying method in mind.

Some elements of the story were drawn from an earlier novelette written by Frances. In *Dead Men Don't Love* (for which Frances used the pseudonym Link Shelton), narrator Joe Manton was jailed for two years for the manslaughter of a man called Penshurst. Manton has been set up, drugged and soused with gin. In *Frails*, Shelton is similarly drugged and set up as a murderer in a pivotal and ironic twist to the plot – the man he is trying to wreak vengeance upon turns the tables, and for a while it appears that Shelton is in more trouble than ever.

In escaping the fate prepared for him by Frisk and his bodyguards, Shelton meets Helen Gaskin and is forced by circumstances to hold her captive. The relationship between Shelton and Helen becomes a central part of the novel, and is another example of Frances's talent for predictive writing. Throughout the "relationship" that develops between Shelton and Helen, Frances creates a tension between the two, where the reader is never sure of Helen's true feelings. She acts as a counterpoint to Shelton's irrational, revenge-driven bitterness, and throughout the novel tries to prevent him from sinking wholesale into retributive violence. She tries to make Shelton see the enormity of what he is doing, telling him, "You've got me on a chain. I guess by now you've got

Frisk on a chain. Did you want to have her on a chain too? What are you going to do? Chain the whole world?"

The modern reader may well be aware of what clinical psychologists call the Stockholm Syndrome. It is named after an event that took place in 1973 at the Sveriges Kreditbank in Normalmstorg, Stockholm. On 23 August, Jan Erik Olsson walked into the bank and tried to hold it up. Police were called immediately, and Olsson opened fire with a sub-machine gun, injuring one officer. Olsson then took four hostages and demanded that his friend, a convict named Clark Olofsson, be brought to the bank as well as three million Krona in cash, guns, bulletproof vests, helmets and a fast car.

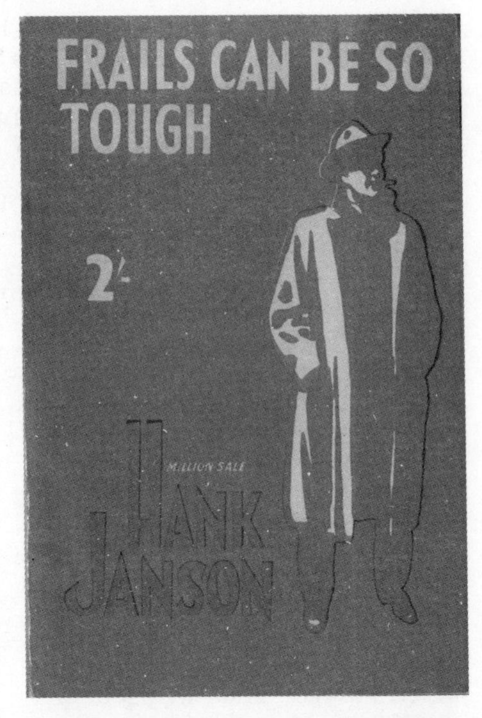

The book as it originally appeared, with its intended Reginald Heade cover artwork censored.

Olsson and Olofsson barricaded themselves into the bank's main vault with their hostages and threatened to kill them if they were not allowed to escape. After a failed attempt by the police to gas the vault, Olsson rigged up snares around the necks of his hostages so that they would be strangled if the same thing was tried again. Later, one of the hostages, Kristin Ehnemark, claimed that she was more terrified by the police than she was of her captors. The police eventually did use tear gas and, after half an hour, the robbers gave themselves up. None of the hostages was injured.

Apart from being one of the first situations of its kind to be broadcast live on television, the bank robbery was remarkable for the actions of the hostages following their release. Olofsson, claiming that his involvement had helped keep the situation calm, was released at a court of appeal after initially being sentenced to imprisonment. He became a friend of Kristin Ehnemark and her family. Olsson was sentenced to ten years, and his telegenic good looks led to many admiring letters from women. He later became engaged to one of his admirers and ended his criminal career. (Olofsson, on the other hand, was involved in a number of other bank robberies and is currently in jail serving a 14-year sentence.)

Frank M. Ochberg, an American professor of psychology, is credited with coining the term "Stockholm Syndrome" in 1978 for what has since become a widely recognised phenomenon (most notoriously in the case of Patti Hearst) in which victims surprisingly bonded with their captors. Over the next few years, the principal factors that lead to this reaction were boiled down to four precursors, which have been summarised thus: the presence of a perceived threat to one's physical or psychological survival and the belief that the abuser would carry out the threat; the presence of a perceived small kindness from the abuser to the victim; isolation from perspectives other than those of the abuser; and the perceived inability to escape the situation.

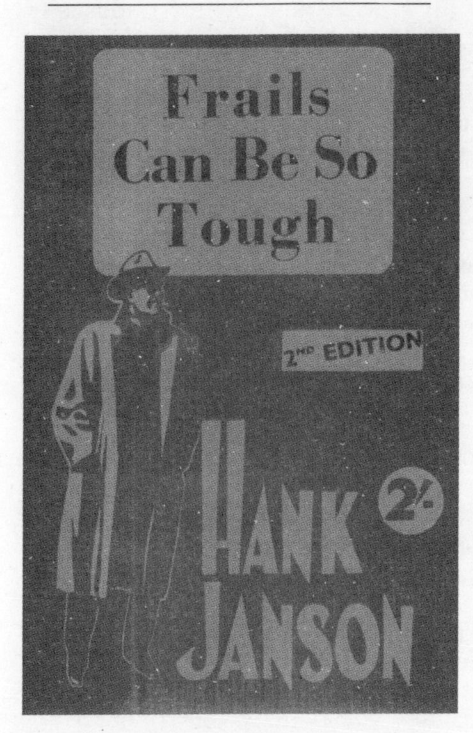

The second edition of the book, published four or five months after the first.

Initially, a bonding with one's captor is a defence mechanism: the captive (sometimes unconsciously) will cooperate and even positively support his or her captor as that will lessen the risk of being injured or killed. The greater peril then becomes the would-be rescuers, who might jeopardize this fragile balance, provoking the captor to carry out his threat.

In *Frails*, published almost 30 years before this bond of interdependence between victim and abuser was named, Stephen Frances created a situation in which the captive Helen Gaskin was held under the precise conditions that we now recognise might result in the unusual relationship she has with Lee Shelton. Shelton threatens her ("So I'm a murderer. Being in for one killing or two makes no difference. I only hang once. What's to stop me bumping you right now?"), imprisons her in a room in an isolated location with a length of chain, foils her attempts to escape until she seemingly becomes aware that her only chance is if Shelton chooses to release her. She becomes penitent and apologetic – "I'm sorry. I lost my temper. I didn't mean to act that way" – and even helps Shelton when he is ill. As a reward, Shelton fetches her handbag and make-up. She begins to see Shelton as a victim rather than a kidnapper, especially when she learns Shelton's background.

Frances had, by instinct and acute observation of human relationships, created and explored the relationship between captive and captor in a way that would have seemed unnatural to most readers, who were more used to their characters being depicted in more black and white terms. Miss Blandish (in *No Orchids For Miss Blandish* by James Hadley Chase) was repulsed by the sexual attentions of psychotic Slim Grisson, and repulsion, pure and simple, is what readers would have expected of Helen Gaskin. What they were given was a far more complex relationship.

Elsewhere in *Frails*, Frances offered a harrowing insight into drug addiction, although that is a subject best left for another introduction, as he explored it more deeply in the next book in the Janson series, *Milady Took The Rap*.

For now, I shall leave you with *Frails Can Be So Tough*. It's a book that, on the surface, has a simple enough plot of revenge. But, like me, I'm sure you will find it a tense thriller that constantly makes you wonder: who exactly is the victim here?

Certainly not the reader.

Steve Holland
Colchester, March 2004

CHAPTER ONE

It was a big, gloomy house that made one think of ghosts and clanking chains. It was gaunt, grim and forbidding, the kinda place you'd glance at and pass by quickly, trying to shrug off the inexplicable cold shudder running down your spine.

The agent didn't like the look of it any more than me. He nosed his car right up to the wrought iron gates, handed me a sickly grin. "I'll just open up," he said.

Those iron gates had been painted green at one time. Now they were a dusty black colour, except where paint had peeled away and dull rust showed. He opened one gate, wedged it back. It squealed protestingly, putting my teeth on edge. The other gate didn't move so easy, dug itself into the gravel path and wedged halfway.

The agent looked at me, grinned reassuringly, like this was all part of his normal letting procedure, wiped perspiration from his forehead with the back of his podgy hand, and gave another heave. He meant business this time.

The gate resisted until the third heave. Then it gave suddenly, tilted crazily as one rusted hinge snapped loose.

He worked hard at it, tried to hold the gate while he opened it to the fullest extent, balanced it carefully in position, hoping I wouldn't notice the hinge had snapped. He bustled back to the car, wiping dirt-smeared hands on a starched white handkerchief, and handed me another of his reassuring smiles. "Just a little oil will fix those. They'll be working as good as new."

I grunted.

He got into gear, started moving up the winding drive that was overgrown with weeds. The borders, which at one time had been neatly mown, were now a wilderness of nettles that reached out, scraped against the car wings as we passed.

He braked when we reached the foot of the cracked steps. I climbed out, went around the car, and climbed the steps to the front door. It was a massive door, which once could have been very impressive. Now it was scorched by sun, paint had flaked away, and the woodwork beneath was damp and grimy.

He came up the steps behind me, fumbling in his pocket for the key and panting slightly with the exertion.

"You don't want to be put off by appearances," he puffed. "It's a good, solid house, well built. Ideal for a man who's got a little money to spend and ideas on development. Very little needed, though. A dash of paint here and there maybe. Been left too long. That's the trouble. But that's in your favour, friend. It means you're going to get it at the right price. The right price for *you*, that is." He chuckled wryly. "The wrong price for *me*, friend."

I grunted, watched as he wrestled with the key. I was interested, wondering whether his strength would give first, or if the key would snap. His perseverance was rewarded. With a grinding protest, the wards of the lock grated across rusted plates, and reluctantly the door swung open.

You could tell by the smell alone it hadn't been inhabited for years. A damp, musty, dirty smell. It was dim inside, too. Dim because of windows coated with dust.

He stepped inside, his shoes creaking so loud it echoed throughout the house, rubbed his hands in satisfaction and chuckled like everything was just as he expected it to be. "Just a little soap and water," he said, with false satisfaction. "It'll be as good as new. All the rooms are large, you'll notice. Isn't this a wonderful reception hall?"

It coulda been at one time. Parquet flooring that should have been waxed and shining beneath the glare of a huge chandelier, a wide sweeping staircase that looped to the first floor. But now the parquet flooring was coated with dust, and in places damp had caused the blocks to erupt. The staircase banisters were so thick with grime I couldn't bear to touch them.

"It's a fine house," he enthused. "A really fine house. Don't you admire the workmanship, the solidity of the building?"

I grunted.

He was looking at me expectantly, his head on one side and his fat face wreathed in a smile. The smile became a fixed grin at my lack of enthusiasm. "I'm glad you agree," he said.

I paced slowly into the lounge. Each step I took echoed up the stairs and around the walls. It was like being in church.

Let me show you the upstairs section," he said eagerly. "All modern conveniences, no expense spared for the comfort of guests."

He went on ahead of me, talking all the time, looking over his shoulder to make sure I was listening. They were nearly all bedrooms on the first floor, all self-contained, with bathrooms and toilets attached. Everywhere was thick dust and an uneasy air of desolation.

"Of course, you're not seeing it at it's best," he pointed out, as we descended. "But I haven't the slightest doubt it could be made really habitable and comfortable."

I grunted.

He'd talked himself out by this time. He was breathing heavily and his slender hopes were steadily dwindling. He didn't find my attitude encouraging. He lost his brightness, asked with a despairing voice: "Is there anything else you'd like to see?"

"Yeah," I said.

He brightened up again. "Everything is open to inspection by our customers." He used a phrase he had used a hundred times before: "Our motto is 'Not satisfied – No deal'"

"What are the cellars like?" I asked.

"Yes, sirree," he said confidently. "Anything you wanna see, you can ..." He broke off, gave me a sharp glance. "What was that you said, friend?"

"The cellars," I said. "I'd like to see the cellars."

He flushed like he was trying to swallow his tongue and was having difficulty.

"You mean ... the cellars!"

I grunted.

He tried to smother his consternation, kinda squared his shoulders. "We're always out to please. What I say is, the satisfied customer is a customer forever. If you'll just follow me this way, friend." He led the way across the hall to a door beneath the stairs. He paused when he reached the door, turned around as though remembering something. "I guess I clean forgot, friend," he apologised. "The electric light's off. You just can't see a thing down there. Maybe it ain't all that important, eh?"

I put my hand in my pocket, pulled out a small flashlight. I showed it to him, switched it on to prove it was working. "This'll help."

He stared at the flashlamp, gulped a coupla times. "Yeah," he croaked. "I guess that'll help."

He went through the door and down the stairs like he was trying to come up at the same time. I pushed past him rudely. "You don't have to come," I said. "I'll look around by myself."

Now he acted differently, couldn't stick close enough to my coat tails. "Of course, the place hasn't been inhabited for some time," he pointed out dolefully. "There's liable to be minor repairs needed. But you expect that, don't you, friend?" His voice was hopeless now, like he'd abandoned all thoughts of letting the joint.

There were two cellars down there, both of them damp and musty. The walls were of brick, coated with green slime from seeping moisture. Evil smelling liquid puddled the concrete floors.

I flashed the torch around, noting the size of the cellar and its dampness. It had the coldness of death, the chilliness of a mortuary refrigerator.

My flashlight showed me other things, too: the rusted waterpipes, which were leaking monotonously, the sewage pipes running through one corner of the cellar, cracked and smelling poisonously. Any house with a basement like this had to be riddled with damp-rot and disease.

I grunted, made my way up the stairs. He followed right behind, muttering about the low cost of new plumbing and the ease with which the work could be undertaken.

I went straight across the hall, straight out through the door and into his car. I was lighting myself a cigarette by the time he'd locked the door of the house, descended the steps and climbed in beside me.

He made one more try. He worked up that uneasy grin, tried to look like he was Father Christmas, and said: "It's a snip for the right man, friend."

I grunted.

He sighed, started the engine, went through the routine of reversing his car. He wasn't a good driver, and it got him sweating. He still went on trying. "Nice situation, too," he said. "Nicely secluded. Not more than twenty minutes from town."

It was not more than twenty minutes if you used a high powered racing car. Then there wouldn't have to be other traffic.

I grunted.

He was heading down the drive now towards the gates. "Shopping facilities are quite good, too, friend," he said. "There's the local stores just ten minutes away. Get anything you want there, friend. Anything at all!"

It'd take nearly half-an-hour to reach what he called the local stores. It was a two-bit general merchant. The kinda place where they're just outta stock of the stuff you need right now, but they will be breaking their necks sell you goods you don't want.

I grunted once more.

We reached the main drag. He hesitated for a moment, like he was gonna get out and close those wrought iron gates. Then he kinda shrugged his shoulders, turned out on to the main drag. I could almost read what was in his mind: *"What's it matter anyway. This fella sitting beside me is the only guy ever likely to think of going in there."*

I sat in moody silence as he pressed his foot down on the throttle, trying to prove his assertion it was only twenty minutes to town. My grim silence got him on edge. His fat face dropped more and more, his eager hopefulness dwindled. Without me saying a word, he concluded it was no deal.

"Where can I drop you, friend?"

"Take me back to your office," I told him.

He gave me a sharp look, eyes brightened again. "Maybe we've got another property that'll interest you."

"Maybe," I breathed. I waited a long while, let the silence between us grow to enormous proportions. Then I said, casually: "How much you asking for that dump, anyway?"

He had a bite and he knew it. A dozen times a day he was talking guys into buying property. He knew every trick of the trade and was a psychologist, too. He moistened his lips with the tip of his tongue, started talking with careful deliberation, choosing his words. "It's this way, friend. That's a firmly constructed, well-made building. Maybe appearances in the first place count against it, but ..."

I interrupted him brutally. "How much do you want for that dump?"

He stared at me haughtily. "I was just about to explain ..."

"I don't want explanations. I've seen what I've seen. I'm asking now. How much do you want for it?"

I was a strange type of fish to him. I was biting. But he didn't wanna scare me away from the bait. He thought a long while and finally mentioned a modest rental, payable a year in advance.

I gave a harsh, contemptuous grunt, looked out from my side of the car like I'd completely lost interest in the deal. About three minutes later, he asked cautiously: "Well, what's your idea of a fair price, friend?"

"Look," I said grimly. "You wanna fair price. Right, you give me a coupla hundred bucks and I'll agree to live in it for a year."

He worked up a chuckle. "You will have your little joke!"

"That's the only way you'll get anybody to live in that joint," I told him. "You'll have to pay them."

"What d'you think's a fair price, friend?" he insisted.

I considered it a long while. Finally I said, with studied firmness: "I'll pay exactly half what you ask, take it on for a year. That's my last word."

He half closed his eyes, shook his head and smiled. "Really, friend," he remonstrated. "You know I couldn't ..."

We were reaching the outskirts of town. "Just draw in there by the bus-stop," I told him. "I'll leave you here."

"No doubt if we discussed the matter ..." he began.

"Pull up," I commanded tersely. "You're overshooting."

He swerved into the kerb, put on his brakes. Almost before the car had stopped, I was opening the door, climbing out.

"Just a minute," he pleaded. "We can talk about this and fix something ..."

"I'm busy," I told him bluntly. "I'm not buying myself an argument."

I was out of the car, walking back towards the bus-stop before he realised it. I stood there, waiting for a bus. Not once did I turn my head and look at him. I figured he'd climb down. All he'd get for that house was a low rental or nothing. He'd prefer the low rental!

Yeah, I was right. He reversed the car, backed right up alongside me. I bent down, poked my head through the window. "Well?" I demanded bluntly.

"Okay," he said morosely. "You win. You get it at your figure."

I opened the door, climbed in beside him. "Let's drive down your office and fix it up," I said. I looked at him thoughtfully. "I still don't know who's being the bigger sucker, you or me."

CHAPTER TWO

Nobody in their right mind would have rented a dump like that to live in. The agent probably figured I was tough as to price but a sap to think of taking on the place at all.

The truth of the matter was the house was exactly what I'd been looking for during the past few weeks. It fitted in with my plans right down to the ground. Right down to the cellar!

I shipped in an army of cleaners from the south side of town, got the place cleaned out, scrubbed, disinfected and rendered relatively habitable. I opened accounts with various stores, bought a little furniture and other things I needed.

I moved in at the end of the week. I had one of the first floor bedrooms furnished and draped. It was a big room with bathroom attached. I furnished it with a large carpet, a comfortable bed and easy chairs. One end of the room I turned into my kitchen, installed a small electric stove and a cupboard to contain the crockery and cooking pans I needed.

Yeah, I know. I'd acted crazy in the first place by taking on that house. Now I was acting even more crazy by furnishing just one room and camping out in it.

But I had my reasons!

Everything was just the way I wanted. I was living in a desolate spot, miles from anywhere. I strenuously resisted the agent's suggestion that he should arrange for a woman to come in and look after me. I wanted nobody around. I was content to do my own shopping, my own cooking, and carry out the task I had set myself, single-handed.

The end of the second week I had my first caller. I was in the cellar at the time. The sound of his knocks re-echoed through the empty house. I swore softly to myself, mounted the stairs to the big hall and opened up.

He was a short, fat guy with an expansive grin. He kept looking over his shoulder apprehensively, and when I opened the door, stared past me as though expecting a raging lion to spring on him.

"Er ... er ... Mr Shelton?"

"Yeah."

He swallowed nervously, loosed his starched collar with his forefinger, and stared past me with apprehensive eyes.

"Something on your mind?" I demanded.

He worked up an uneasy grin. "That's right," he said nervously. "The dog. Place I called at coupla weeks ago, I got bitten. Had to have it cauterised." He peered at me anxiously. "That means burnt," he explained. "It's very painful."

"Quit worrying," I told him. "No dogs here."

His mouth widened. "No dogs!"

I frowned at him. "Say, who are you, anyway?"

"You've never met me, Mr Shelton. I thought I'd call and see you." He swallowed nervously, peered over my shoulder again. "You're sure about the dogs, aren't you?"

"No dogs," I said irritably. "What d'you want?"

He fumbled in his pocket, produced a slip of paper, which he unfolded carefully. "I'm the ironmonger," he explained. "Hawkins, the ironmonger. I was passing this way and thought I'd drop in about this small account of yours."

I widened the door. "Better come in a minute. I'll write you a cheque."

He stood in the extensive, bare entrance hall, looking around with surprise in his eyes. The house was empty and bleak, the way it had been when I first took it, except it was cleaned up.

I took the invoice from his hand, glanced at it. "Hang on a moment," I told him. "I'll get you a cheque."

I had to go upstairs for my cheque-book. When I got downstairs again, he was looking around as though mystified. Part of his interest was in the bricks and cement bags over by the cellar-door.

"Making alterations to the cellar?" he asked. What he really meant was: *"What the hell you gonna use those bricks for?"*

I glanced at them casually. "Chimney alterations," I told him. "Builders coming in some time next week."

He nodded his head understandingly. "I guess there's lots of alterations you'll need around here." The wind blowing along an empty corridor upstairs caused a door to slam loudly. His head jerked, he stared towards the stairway apprehensively.

"Just the wind," I said.

He licked his lips. "About them dogs," he said. "Are you gonna have many?"

He puzzled me. "What dogs?"

"Have to watch out for them," he warned. "Doctor was telling me how dangerous hydrophobia is. Have to have it cauterised."

"What dogs?" I repeated.

His eyes gleamed with sudden interest. "Say," he said. "You ain't figuring on having something really fierce, a lion or a tiger or something?"

I stared at him doubtfully. He didn't look crazy, but he certainly talked that way. "I've gotta think about it," I said cautiously.

He grinned, winked one eye. "Something special, eh, Mr Shelton? I knew it. Immediately I saw your order for those chains, I knew it was gonna be fierce dogs or something special. Maybe you're an animal trainer or something, Mr Shelton?"

I got it then. I hadn't been taking any chances. I'd bought all I'd needed and more. All those chains and padlocks musta got him puzzled. At first he'd pictured a vicious dog straining on those chains. Now he was getting even more exaggerated ideas.

"I'm a strange kinda guy," I told him. "I don't like folks bothering me much. You were right first time. I'm having half-a-dozen huskies sent from Canada. You know what they're like, vicious brutes. Ideal for keeping away inquisitive folks. You need a lotta chains with them kinda animals."

He smiled with satisfaction. "I knew it was dogs," he said triumphantly. That scared look came back into his face suddenly. "You ain't got any here now, have you?"

I grinned reassuringly. "Not due till next week. You don't have to worry."

That's fine," he said. "That's real fine." He looked at me anxiously. "Just one thing, Mr Shelton," he asked. "I don't want to be any worry to you at all. So any time you order anything, maybe you could send the cheque by post, eh?"

"Sure," I said. "I'll send it by post."

When he'd gone, I went back to the cellar. It sure was hard work. I'd rigged up an electric lamp to work by. I'd hacked holes in thick brickwork, was busy now cementing in iron staples to which were fastened long lengths of stout chain. The final job would be bricking in the doorway.

But I wasn't ready for that yet!

I contented myself with laying the three lower rows of bricks, omitting a coupla bricks on the very lowest row, leaving a gap just big enough to allow passage of a food pan.

Yeah, it was hard work. But I was enjoying it. Because every moment of that sweating, gruelling labour was in a sense a reward. It was giving me something I wanted deep down inside me. It was the arranging of the stage props for the final act. It was – the payoff!

I was in no hurry. I'd waited so long, I could easily wait much longer. I spent another fortnight completing the work, making sure everything was exactly the way I wanted it. Only when I was quite satisfied my setting was perfect did I begin the next stage of my plan.

Even after paying the rent of that house for a year in advance, and the cost of the extras, I still had dough in the bank. I bought myself a new suit, silk shirts and an expensive watch. I bought a new leather wallet, stuffed it with dollar bills. When I inspected myself carefully in the mirror, my reflection showed a tall, slim, fashionably and expensively dressed guy with neatly combed black hair and – I guess I am entitled to say it, since other folk have – expressive brown eyes.

I looked at my watch. It was nine o'clock. Just the time folks were thinking about dinner.

I put on my fedora, placed a new, light overcoat on my arm and went out to the garage. I used a smart little blue coupe. But it wasn't smart enough for playing my part. I decided to walk until I could pick up a bus into town. It had it's advantages. If I ran my head into trouble this evening, the cops wouldn't be able to trace me by my car licence number.

Yeah, that was the funny thing about it. For years I'd been planning to do just this thing. And tonight, for the first time, I'd thought of what the cops could do about it.

After years of planning, the cops weren't gonna stop me now. I walked down the drive, turned out on to the main drag and set off for town. It was a nice evening, just right for a stroll.

It had to be just right. Because right now the curtain was going up and the play was beginning.

CHAPTER THREE

I dropped off the bus at town centre, called a cab and directed him to the Sugar Loaf.

I hadn't been in town for years. But I'd studied the facts that concerned me so thoroughly, there wasn't a thing I didn't know about the Sugar Loaf.

It was a swell joint, frequented by swanky folk who had the kinda dough it needs to visit a joint like that.

I deposited my coat with the peroxided, fluffy-haired blonde who looked after the cloakroom, and flashed her a big tip. It earned me a broad smile, an engaging twinkle of blue eyes and the smarmy attention of the hovering and watching head waiter.

I crossed his palm with crackling paper money, like I'd been doing it all my life, before even asking him for a good table. He figured he was on a good thing, showed plenty of deference, clapped his hands smartly so that waiters were fluttering around me like vultures around a freshly-killed animal.

It was a classy joint. Only me and two other guys were not wearing tails. All the dames were in evening dress, backless and strapless evening gowns that cost plenty and were plenty attractive. I'd never before in one place and at one time seen so much bosom. And these were real high-class bosoms, ornamented with gleaming, flashing sapphires and glistening pearls.

Any gunman with a fancy for a little excitement could have made a haul merely by flashing a gun and circulating around the guests with a large sack to collect the spoils.

I ordered carefully, choosing the best and the most expensive. A coupla tables away, a young guy was acting host to two dames. He paid plenty of attention to one of them, left the other in the cold. When he escorted his choice to the dance floor, the lonely dame glanced around soulfully, caught my eye, looked away quickly and embarrassedly. A few moments later, just a little too casually, she moved around so I could get full focus on her plunging neckline. If she'd leaned forward just a little more, I'd have seen down to the soles of her shoes. It was a great temptation. It needed only a hastily scribbled note passed to her by the waiter to get her curves pressed up tight against me on the dance-floor.

But I wasn't here on pleasure. I was here on business. I paid attention to what I was eating, wondered just how much information I'd be getting later, and what use I could make of it. Next time I glanced at the dame, she'd lost all restraint, was gazing at me soulfully. She smiled sadly when my eyes met hers.

They were nice eyes, brown and pouting, and I wasn't in all that hurry. I'd waited years. I could wait just a little longer. I scribbled on the back of a menu, caught a waiter's eye.

She didn't even read it. She knew what it was. She nodded to me as the waiter put the menu in her hand. I got up, crossed to her. "Would you care to dance?"

She flashed me a dazzling smile as she led the way to the dance-floor. The band was playing a slow, sentimental foxtrot. As soon as I put my arms around her, she went right into a clinch, kinda went to sleep on me while she was standing up, her body moulding into mine from chest to knee. She was clinging, smouldering dynamite, every line and curve of her body moulding into mine so faithfully it felt she was naked. She almost was at that! The silkiness of her skin imparted an electric tingle to my fingers that was disconcerting. I dropped my hand lower to escape the disturbing effect of it. That dress sure was backless. I stopped lowering my hand when it had reached a point where it would be improper to place it any lower. And my fingers were still being electrified. I swallowed, began to sweat slightly, and slid my fingers upwards again. She gave a pleased little sigh, wriggled herself deliciously and did some more body-moulding. Her cheek was resting on my chest, her eyes were closed and her body only moved with mine. If I'd have stopped dancing, she'd have stayed right the way she was. She spoke for the first time. "That was nice," she whispered contentedly.

Maybe it was. But I had a busy evening before me. All I'd planned on doing was dancing with her. She acted like she had certain other plans.

I was relieved yet disappointed when the dance finished and the lights came on. She clung to my arm, squeezed it meaningfully, looked up at me with frankly inviting eyes. Somehow her chest nudged me a coupla times.

Then we were back at her table, and she was introducing me. "This is my brother, Captain Foster, and his fiancee, Emily Dean."

"My name's Shelton," I told them. "Lee Shelton." I looked at her enquiringly.

"Diane," she said. "Diane Foster."

"Miss?"

Her eyes smiled roguishly. "Miss," she said, with a slight emphasis.

The brother and his fiancee were so wrapped up in each other that they'd already forgotten about us. I gave a polite little bow, returned to my table. Diane sat back in her chair, stared at me with frankly approving eyes. She was eager and expectant, all ready for the next dance.

But she had to control her impatience. The lights went out all over the restaurant, spotlights played on the dance-floor for the cabaret troupe. And what those high-class guests with their diamond necklaces and low-cut dresses put on show was as nothing in comparison with the tastefully revealed charms of the cabaret girls. They enacted a South Sea Island folk dance, which the programme described as being hundreds of years old. The name of it was unpronounceable, but the programme thoughtfully gave the translation - *The dance that makes you think about it.*

The six dancers were certainly not Polynesian. But they had shining black hair and eyes, and what passed for South Sea Island costumes. In a night club, that is – certainly not in the South Sea Islands. The costumes were brief but spectacular. Long necklaces of small sea shells drooped across their breasts, and strips of brightly-coloured satin were strained tautly around their loins, like embryo bikini bathing shorts. The band played slowly at first, mostly guitars and drums. With their first, easy, graceful movements, the dancers made those shell necklaces sway revealingly. Then, as the dance got into its pace, you could see those girls musta worked at learning it. It wasn't only their feet that danced, it was their entire bodies. They used their eyes and faces expressively, their arms were graceful and meaningful, their bodies supple and rippling. It wasn't just a dance. It was primitive human emotion expressed in vitalised rhythm and movement. And it wasn't movement that could be learned, It was movement that could be acquired only by years of study and requiring deep feeling and understanding.

The guitars became louder, the drummers beat more passionately, and I couldn't move my eyes from those dames as they swayed their hips, rolled their bellies sensuously, each full circular movement completed with a sharp, urgent forward thrust. There was a mad, magnetic ecstasy in the dancing, which heated my blood, made me lean forward watching intently, even panting slightly myself. The dance became faster and faster, wilder and wilder. The dame nearest me danced like she was possessed, every sharp, forward thrust of her body flicking the slender sea-shell necklace high off her breasts. All the time, her hips and her belly were rolling at an ever-increasing speed, the muscles of her sides, back and thighs were jerking unceasingly. They danced madly, faster and faster, continuing so long I became anxious for them, afraid they would crack beneath the strain of it. Yet still they continued perfect with precision and amazing stamina. The girl nearest me was twirling madly, her body jerking seductively with the rhythm of the drums. She was overcome by the rhythmic frenzy of the dance. I was beginning to feel that way myself.

Then, very gradually, the music began to slow and die away. As it slowed, the dancers lost their frenzy, eased down until, with legs parted and half-bent and arms gracefully extended above their heads, the only movement they made was the slow, sensuous rolling of their bellies.

Even that movement died in perfect harmony with the music.

For a moment there was awed silence. Then came the applause. Overwhelming applause. The dancer nearest me was smiling, keeping her lips parted as she panted and tried not to show it. I could tell she was breathless by the way her breasts heaved. It wasn't surprising. She sure had worked at it. Her body glistened, the red satin strip around her loins wore a dark sweat-patch, and beads of perspiration trickled down her smooth thighs.

That dance was a remarkable exhibition of controlled movement, precision and rhythm. But it was more than that. It lived up to its name. It certainly made me think about it.

It wasn't only me it affected that way. When the lights went on, Diane was looking at me again. And there was no doubt as to what was in her mind!

I danced with her twice more. The second time, she suggested we might go some place quiet and have a drink. There was conflict waging inside me. My plan won. I told her we'd make it some other time, escorted her back to her table and called the waiter over to me.

I spoke in his ear, confidentially. "I wanna little excitement."

"Would you like me to recommend a theatre or a show, sir?"

I looked at him meaningfully. "Don't give me that!"

He went away, came back with the head waiter – the guy I'd tipped lavishly. "What is it you want, sir?"

I stared at him levelly, half-lowered one eyelid. "Just a little excitement."

"I'm afraid I don't understand, sir."

I'd carefully slipped another lavish tip into his palm. "Do I look like a cop?" I demanded. "There isn't a table in Chicago or New York I haven't played. Have I gotta die of boredom on account I'm a newcomer in town?"

He stared at me thoughtfully. I grinned back. He asked, cautiously: "Is there anybody you know? Somebody who would recommend you?"

"I hit town today," I told him. "I made a few enquiries around. Got this name every time. Seems like the whole town knows about it."

"We have to be careful," he pointed out.

I leaned forward, said in a low voice: "Listen, bud. I have to be careful, too. I'd hate to have my name tied in on a raid."

He thought about it for maybe another five seconds. Then he said, with decision: "I guess it's okay."

"Where do I go?"

He nodded cautiously across the restaurant towards a corridor labelled "Smoking Room." "About five minutes' time," he said. "Go straight through and I'll meet you the other end."

I got my cheque, settled the bill with a flourish and another large tip. When I got up, Diane was watching me with pained eyes, brow furrowed with disappointment. It was almost as though she was saying *"You can't go. Not now!"*

I hated breaking it up between us. But I had my business to attend to. I nodded to her sharply, turned on my heel quickly, because she looked like she was gonna get up and speak to me, and threaded my way through the tables.

A little later, I made my way to the "Smoking Room," loitered for a moment, and then passed on along the corridor. It was a long corridor with two right-angle turnings. At the far end, the head waiter was waiting for me. He stood in front of a plain, unvarnished door. He gave a quick succession of knocks that were obviously a code. A flap in the door opened and two eyes peered through. "Let this guy in," said the head waiter. "He's okay."

As the door opened, I slipped another large bill in his hand. It was policy to keep him sweet. I didn't know when I'd be needing him again.

It was a large room, well-lighted and very, very full. I elbowed my way over to the roulette table, took up a position behind a dame with a stack of chips in front of her. She was a young dame, not more than twenty, who looked like she'd been over-dieting. Her shoulder-blades stood out like the ribs of a starved horse, and her arms were long and thin. So thin it was incredible. The bodice of her dress was supported by a diamond collar, which would have kept a working man and his family for a lifetime. I stood close, looked over her shoulder to watch her play. She had a plunging neckline. It extended to her waist, where a slender girdle was fastened with a diamond-studded clip. I don't know what she thought fashion did for her. All that plunging neckline advertised was her prominent, fleshless chest bones. Apart from that, she was as flat as a board – maybe a little flatter.

But the really interesting thing about that dame was her attitude. I could feel her all tightened up inside, taut like a drum. I could feel the eager desperateness inside her when she counted chips onto a square. Then it was like I could feel her going around and around with the roulette wheel, the sharp click of the ball an echo inside her, plucking at her nerve-strings, so she was hovering between life and death during the long seconds it took for the wheel to slow and the ball to fall in a numbered slot.

The croupier called: "Thirty-six. Red."

I felt the heavy sag inside her. The weight that drew her down, sucked at her life's blood. It lasted while the croupier's rake reached out, scooped in the chips on the table. Then there was eager desperateness inside her once more as she reached out her bony arm, pushed more chips onto the same square.

I glanced around. Most of the folks there had that same eager, reckless glint in their eyes. They were dope addicts, transported from the depths to the heights on the twist of a wheel, their hopes plunging as fortune slipped between their fingers, then soaring to the heavens as chips piled up in front of them. Never did they have the gumption to quit when the going was good.

I went to the cashier, exchanged all the dough I had for gambling chips. I went back to the roulette table, squeezed in alongside the bony dame.

Luck was running dead against her. The pile of chips in front of her was steadily diminishing. Her face was white, except for two red spots high up on her cheeks. But each time she pushed more chips onto a square, that same eager, desperate light gleamed in her eyes.

Maybe in Monte Carlo and other resorts where gambling is permitted, the wheel is operated honestly. After all, the odds are always in favour of the bank, although it may be only for a small percentage. But it was a dime to a grand that in an illegal gambling joint like this, the wheel was fixed so the house couldn't lose, whatever happened.

I had a theory about fixed wheels. A very simple theory, which I reckoned to try out at some time. You've got to understand the point of view of the guy who's running the wheel to understand my theory. Once you put yourself in his shoes, realize what pays him best, you can't go wrong.

Figure yourself as a croupier seated at the head of table, with the suckers carefully placing their chips and hoping they're gonna win a fortune. They've finished laying their stakes now, and you're getting ready to twirl the wheel. You give one last look around. Everybody's placed their stake on the board. You shout, in a loud voice, "No more bets," and start that wheel revolving.

Now comes your testing point. You've got to be an expert mathematician, and you've got to be able to size up the table in a flash. All kinds of bets are placed, some folks betting red will win, others betting black will win. These bets only pay off evens. There are some folk who like a real gamble. They're the guys who bet on just one number. If that one number turns up, they get paid thirty-six times their original stake. There are other folks who like a gamble but are more cautious. They bet on a group of four numbers, which pays off nine to one. Other folks bet on groups of twelve, six or two numbers. They take their choice of bet, select the odds they want.

But back to the croupier. He's got it all weighed up. He's studied these tables for years. And as the wheel turns, he's calculating ferociously. Not everybody can win. Only some people can win. And the croupier doesn't care who the winners are. All he's concerned is that the bank shall receive more in stake money than it pays out in odds. So his quick eye notices that, all told, there's a thousand dollars on the table betting that red will turn up, another five hundred saying the number will be over eighteen. A further five hundred bucks is betting the number will be an odd number.

That's two thousand bucks betting the number will be red, odd and over eighteen.

Almost at the same moment, he calculates that if the number is under eighteen, black and an even number, he'll have to pay to the winners only a matter of fifteen hundred bucks.

It doesn't matter when and how he operates the mechanism of that crooked wheel. That's a factual detail. All I know is, that if the game is crooked, without a doubt the number is going to be under eighteen, black and even.

So that's the croupier's set-up. He plays the table for the house, making sure that whoever wins, the house doesn't lose.

As for me, the player, what do I do? Well, it's simple. I wait till the last moment before laying my bet. I play a corpse hand. I bet the opposite way to the folks who are making the high stakes. The only drawback is, I have to bet small. If I betted big, the wheel would be turned against me instead of against them.

I could have done it with the bony dame. She was backing heavily, losing heavily. I could have corpsed every move she made, bet dead opposite to her and won every time she lost.

But I hadn't come to make a fortune. I'd come to lose dough. So I backed the thin dame's hunches, paralleled her bets to a smaller extent.

I didn't lose all the time. That would have been too obvious. Once in a while, the croupier played it straight, so the bank didn't always win.

But giving the suckers an occasional win was good psychology. To see a pile of chips pushed over to you renewed hope, gave an indication losses could be recovered, induced folks to plunge even more deeply.

A coupla hours steady playing saw the end. I lost my last chip the same time as the thin dame lost the last of her dough. When her last chip was scooped in by the croupier's rake, she sat staring at the board like she couldn't believe her eyes. There were plenty of other folk anxious to play, and the croupier's eyes were on her. With a white face, and an unquenched thirst to recover her losses still gleaming in her eyes, she quit her chair, fingered her collar and glanced around.

I was right behind her when she went to the cashier. She didn't say anything. She just took off the diamond necklace, placed it on the desk in front of him.

He looked from her to the necklace calculatingly. He had a large cigar stuck in the corner of his mouth. He spoke through it, choosing his words. "What d'you want me to do with it, lady?"

"What will you advance me on it?"

He took his time about replying. "Sorry, lady. We don't make advances."

She sounded kinda desperate. "But you must. I've lost so much money and I must have a chance to get it back. If you'll only advance me ..."

He interrupted her with brutal finality. "We don't advance money on jewellery any time, ma'am." He paused, watched the warring emotions reflected in her eyes. He added, just a little too casually: "If you wanna sell, lady. That's different, see!"

"Sell!" She'd never considered selling it. She only wanted to hock it. "I couldn't do that!" she said, horrified at the idea.

He shrugged his shoulders. "That's all I can do, lady."

She picked up the necklace, left him slowly and reluctantly. Her head was bowed and her shoulders drooped. I moved up to talk to him. He was watching the dame, that calculating look still in his eyes. And he was right. Because she was coming back.

"How much ... I mean what would you ...?"

"You wanna sell, lady?" he asked bluntly.

"What would I get for it?"

He shrugged his shoulders. "That ain't my department. But if you wanna sell, you'll have to see Mr Frisk. He makes his own valuations, does his own buying."

"I wouldn't want to sell unless I could be sure to get a good price," she faltered.

"Mr Frisk buys cheap," he told her frankly.

"Could I ... I mean ... when I win some money, could I buy it back?"

He chuckled grimly. "You discuss that with Mr Frisk. Maybe you could buy it back. At a price!"

She looked over her shoulder at the table, feverishly. She said, like she was talking to herself: "I'm sure I'm on a winning run. It's due up any time, now."

"You wanna see Mr Frisk, lady?" he interrupted rudely. "Do you?"

She hesitated, torn with indecision. Then it seemed to burst out without her being able to control her voice. "Yes please," she said quickly. "I'd like to see Mr Frisk. Right now, if you please."

He signalled to a guy in evening dress who was lounging in a chair, smoking a cigarette. Even in evening dress, the guy still managed to look flashy. The cashier jerked his thumb towards the dame. "She wants to see the boss."

The fella flashed her a grin that was too wide, jerked his head: "This way, lady."

I watched him push his way across the room with the dame following behind him. He went across to the far side, pushed through a door marked "Private". A voice interrupted me. A harsh voice.

"What's on your mind, bud?"

I looked at the cashier. His eyes were hard and stony. I worked up a grin. "What's a guy do about getting credit!"

"Nothing," he said flatly. "You just don't get it."

"I'm betting with the lady," I told him. "I'm sure we're on a winning run. I wanna back my hunch, but I've run out of ready. What d'you suggest?"

"Go home," he said baldly. "Money's the only thing that counts around here. If you ain't got it, we don't lend it."

"How about a cheque?"

He thought about that. "Some cheques are fine," he said. "Others aren't so good. They stretch."

I drew myself up, got an indignant note into my voice.

"I'm not in the habit of issuing bouncing cheques."

"You oughta meet some of the guys I've met."

"You're being offensive," I told him. "Are you willing to cash a cheque or not?"

My indignation amused him. He leaned forward across the desk, clasped his hands and grinned up at me. "Sure," he said agreeably. "We cash cheques. Mr Frisk cashes them. But it's a lotta trouble. He takes a risk, too. He charges twenty per cent for the facility he gives you."

"That's fantastic," I burst out. "Twenty per cent extra for cashing a cheque! I've never heard anything like it before."

He still smiled at me agreeably. "That's all right, fella. You go home like I told you. You don't wanna hang around here."

I swallowed hard. "I'm just on a winning run," I said. "If I can get just a little dough ..."

"Make up your mind, bud," he invited. "D'you wanna cheque cashed?"

I hesitated, fought a battle with myself and then yielded. "Okay," I said. "I'll cash a cheque."

The agreeable smile was still on his face, but his eyes changed. They became hard and menacing. "Just one more thing, bud," he said. "That cheque had better not bounce. If it does, you'll bounce even higher! We kinda take a dislike to guys who try pulling a fast one."

"My cheques are okay," I said weakly.

"It's your last chance to back out, bud. If you ain't got dough in the bank, back out now. It'll save you a lotta grief."

"My cheque's good," I said.

He nodded with satisfaction. "You'll have to wait a few minutes," he said. "Mr Frisk will be available any moment now."

I waited about five minutes. At the end of that time, the bony dame was back with that same eager, hopeful look in her eyes. She handed the cashier a slip of paper and his face creased in a wide grin when he saw it. "He sure herded you close on that sale," he commented.

That was all I had time to hear, because the guy with the flashing smile was steering me across the room to that far door, the one marked "Private."

He opened the door, pushed straight inside without knocking. I followed close on his heels. We were in a long, well-lighted corridor. He led the way, and I followed to the far end. This time he paused, knuckled the next door with respect. It had painted on it in smooth gilt letters the name, "Mr J J Frisk."

A muffled voice sounded through the panels. The flashy-smile guy opened the door, stood on one side and motioned me through.

I took a deep breath. Everything was going fine. It was working just the way I'd planned. Everything was coming to a head now. Because right now I was about to meet the man I'd been waiting to meet for fifteen years.

CHAPTER FOUR

His phone bell rang at the same time I entered. He picked up the receiver, began talking into it, and motioned me to sit opposite him.

As I sat in that comfortable, hide-bound chair, I watched him across his wide, oak desk; studied him with a kinda scientific detachment. At the same time, I tried to suppress the fluttery feeling in my belly.

He was just the same as I'd remembered him; changed in little ways, of course. Then he had been forty. Now he was fifty-five. But he was in excellent condition. His hair was smooth and black, glossy and neatly parted. It receded further back on the temples than when I had last seen him. But he hadn't one grey hair!

His skin was smooth and unwrinkled. Just think of that! Not one wrinkle in his high forehead. Maybe that was on account he didn't worry. He never worried about anything. Or, to put it in another way, he never cared a tinker's cuss about anybody. The only thing that counted in his life was himself.

His eyes were brown and kindly. As he spoke into the telephone, they had a thoughtful, faraway expression in them. If you didn't know as much as I did, you'd figure right away he'd be a good guy to dress up as Father Christmas and hand out toys to the kiddies.

That would be one Christmas you could bet on the kids being disappointed.

There was still that little cleft in his chin. He still had that habit of fingering it while he talked. He was doing it now.

Yeah, he was just the same as I remembered him, even after all these years. He was handsome, sleek, and well-dressed. He looked kindly and human. But he was a ruthless fiend, a man who would do anything for his only god – money!

That fluttery feeling in my belly was quietening now. So far, he'd hardly given me a glance. I was scared he'd recognise me. If he did, my careful planning would be wasted. Even if he didn't recognise me, I had a tough job ahead. From this point onwards, I had no specific plan except to ingratiate myself with him somehow and choose my right moment.

He finished talking, replaced the receiver, and as he did so, his eyes slipped across the table towards me. I knew a moment of fear, dropped my own eyes. I found myself staring at the bony dame's necklace. Almost at once, his delicately manicured hand reached forward, swept the necklace into his desk drawer. His quiet, modulated voice said, whimsically: "A little souvenir."

I had to look at him. I had to know if he recognised me. I stared levelly into those kindly brown eyes, saw in them only speculation.

"You're Mr Frisk?" I asked.

"What can I do for you?"

I grinned ruefully. "The numbers weren't running for me on your table."

He tut-tutted. "You didn't lose too heavily, I hope?" His eyes and voice suggested it would break his heart if I lost too much.

"Less than I can afford to lose," I said. "I wanna lose a little more, give that table a thorough beating."

He smiled understandingly, nodded his head and made a tent of his fingers. "You wish to obtain a little ready money. Is that it?"

"The cashier said you'd change a cheque."

Momentarily his eyes hardened. Then once again his eyes were kindly. "My cashier explained that we are always willing to be of service – for a consideration?"

"He told me," I grunted. "He also threatened what would happen if the cheque bounced."

If he'd been the nice, kindly guy he looked, such a remark shoulda knocked him off his perch with surprise. But he took it easily, smiled with those kindly eyes and nodded his head approvingly. "I prefer my clients to understand fully the situation," he purred.

"You'll cash a cheque then?"

"Just a few details first, Mr ...?" He paused enquiringly.

I hesitated. The question caught me on the hop. I said, "My name's Martin. John Martin. I'm stopping at the Oxbell Hotel."

He noted it in careful, precise handwriting on a memo pad. My heart was in my mouth. I thought maybe he'd try checking at the hotel. He didn't. He just said, coolly: "How much ready cash do you want?"

"A grand will cover me, I guess."

He nodded, opened a drawer in his desk and pulled out another pad. This was printed, used internally between him and the cashier. I watched him pencil in the amount. 1,000 dollars. As he initialled it, he said: "Just let me have a cheque for twelve hundred dollars, will you please?"

I had a cheque book ready on a bank in Nebraska. I wrote carefully, twelve hundred dollars to be paid to J J Frisk. I almost went wrong, almost signed my own name on the cheque. I remembered in time, signed John Martin.

He took the cheque, studied it carefully, then placed it in his desk drawer and handed me the memo. "The cashier will give you the markers you require."

Now I was stuck. Somehow I had to get in well with him, manoeuvre him some place where I could get him alone. I could do it only by having his confidence, otherwise I'd be in trouble with the two bodyguards who shadowed him wherever he went.

"You're kinda interested in business deals, Mr Frisk?" I said bluntly.

His kindly eyes studied me thoughtfully. "Who isn't?"

"I've got some pretty big irons in some very hot fires," I told him. "Can I get you interested?"

"Could do," he admitted reluctantly. "It depends on the size of the irons and the heat of the fires."

I took out a cigarette, lit it slowly and breathed through my nostrils. I took a long time about it. Then I said, slowly: "It's a deal worth a coupla hundred grand."

Not a muscle of his face moved. "That's big money, Mr Martin."

"I'm a big guy," I said. "I'm interested in big money. Aren't you?"

He leaned forward across the table; his face was quite close to mine now. "What's your proposition?"

I breathed more smoke through my nostrils, grinned, gestured around the office. "Hardly the place to talk about it."

The skin over his cheekbones tautened. "I transact all my business here."

I grinned at him cheekily. "Microphones under the desk? Every conversation recorded? No, Mr Frisk. What I've got up here" – I tapped my forehead – "means real money. I tell part of it at the right time to the right person. I'm too smart to have somebody heating my irons for me."

He studied me thoughtfully. I stared back at him. I wished I knew what he was thinking. One thing was sure. He was interested. If I could play this right, he'd maybe walk into my trap.

Yet all my careful planning for revenge that had been smouldering inside me for fifteen years was suddenly shattered. Interrupted rudely and abruptly by the office door smashing inwards under the impact of two struggling bodies.

I scrambled out of my chair, stared in surprise as they rolled on the floor. One of them was the flashy-smile guy, the other was an older guy, a grey-haired fella about fifty.

"What the hell ...?" roared Frisk. He, too, was on his feet, glaring balefully as they struggled. A third man came running in, a broad-shouldered guy with the face of an ex-pugilist. He didn't hesitate, launched himself on top of the struggling pair.

His appearance made all the difference. In less than a minute, all three of them were on their feet again. The flashy-smile guy was rumpled, dusty and flushed. The broad-shouldered hood was smiling with satisfaction as he scientifically twisted the older guy's arm. The older guy was poised on tip-toe, strained there by the agony of his twisted arm.

Frisk stared at him. "How the devil did you get in here, Manton?" he demanded. At the same time, he motioned urgently to flashy-smile, who obediently closed the door.

The old guy gritted his teeth, moaned piteously. "You're breaking my arm."

Frisk ordered: "Okay, Jenks. Let him go. Watch him, though."

Jenks released him. But before he did so, he ran his hands over the old man, dug down in his pocket and produced a revolver. With a meaningful gesture, he leaned forward, slid it across the desk towards Frisk.

Frisk picked up the gun, held it pointing at Manton and smiled grimly. "Have you got a licence for this?"

I got my first real good look at Manton then. I saw he was grey-haired, haggard and with the red-rimmed eyes of an habitual drinker. But there was a kinda pathetic nobility about him as he squared his shoulders, stared straight at Frisk. "Where's my daughter?" he demanded, and at the same time his hands and face began to work. His voice crackled hysterically. "Where's my daughter, you damned swine?" he yelled. "What have you done with her? What have you done with my daughter!"

Frisk's eyes narrowed ominously. He took a deep breath. "You'd better get this straight for the last time, Manton," he said coldly. "I don't know where your daughter is, and I don't wanna know. Is that understood? Now get outta here. And understand. If I ever find you around here again, you won't get off so light."

Manton's hands and face worked so terribly I was scared he was gonna hurl himself at Frisk. But the broad-shouldered Jenks grasped him firmly by the arm, his hard, cruel fingers digging into flesh. Manton licked his lips nervously. Frisk said, contemptuously: "Get him outta here, will ya?"

Jenks dragged at Manton, pulled him away from the desk. Manton's eyes flamed and his face contorted in anger. "You can't treat me this way," he yelled, and he twisted with unexpected strength, tore himself free from Jenks and tried to launch himself across the desk at Frisk.

Flashy-smile reached him in time, grasped him by the back of the collar. "Cut it out, bud," he rasped, and there was an evil tone in his voice that belied the softness of his features. The hand that wasn't grasping Manton's collar was jamming a .45 hard into Manton's backbone.

Just about the most uncomfortable thing you can feel digging in your backbone is the muzzle of a revolver. When that hard iron ring is digging into your spine, it makes you stop dead in your tracks and start thinking. Because in that moment you're face to face with death, realize your life is dangling on a thread as slender as your spinal cord. And your spinal cord can be shattered in a split second by the swift tightening of a finger.

Manton kinda froze. He was scared. He sure was a mixed-up guy. Anger, fear, fury and rage were boiling around inside him. It looked like the fear was winning, because when flashy-smile tightened his grip on Manton's collar, he curled his lips, snarled in a low, menacing voice: "I'll get you for this, Frisk. I'll get you sometime, somehow!"

"Come on, bud," snarled flashy-smile. He jerked hard on Manton's collar, twirled him around, propelled him towards the door. Jenks stood at the door, ready to open it, poised like he was gonna add his boot to Manton's rear. Frisk watched with hard, thoughtful eyes, still holding the revolver carelessly.

Nobody expected another squawk outta Manton. He was outnumbered three to one, there was a revolver pointing at him and he was no physical match for the two hoods who were escorting him off the premises.

Maybe it was because nobody was expecting it that Manton nearly succeeded. As Jenks opened the door, flashy-smile momentarily released his grip. It was enough for Manton. With another spurt of that unexpected vitality, he spun around, smashed his fist into flashy-smile's face, and in the same moment, chopped with the edge of his palm on the back of flashy-smile's gun hand.

It all happened so quickly that, before I'd taken it in, flashy-smile was reeling backwards, his gun was slithering across the floor and Manton was diving after it.

I'd never have thought Manton had so much speed in him. He grasped the gun, scrambled to his feet, pointed it with trembling fingers at Frisk. His eyes were wild, his hands trembling and his face working. "Where's my daughter?" he gasped. "I've gotta know. What have you done with my daughter?"

Jenks was poised ready to spring. But he didn't. The reason was clear. A .45 bullet trembled on the end of Manton's finger, and it was headed straight for Frisk. And did that finger tremble!

It was a tricky situation. A sudden movement by Jenks might easily cause Manton to fire. I had only to look at Frisk's face to realize he knew that better than anybody. He was worth looking at. If you wanted a study in sheer blue funk, a photograph of Frisk would have made a perfect specimen.

I've seen guys scared before. I've seen brave guys scared and I've seen cowards scared. But never have I seen anybody as scared as Frisk in that moment. His face was dead-white, his forehead gleaming with cold sweat, his lips trembling and sheer, stark panic in his eyes.

Manton saw his fear, rejoiced in his own, new-found power. He jabbed with the gun, got more menace into his voice. "I'm giving you one more chance, Frisk," he gritted. "Tell me where my daughter is. Just one more chance." But he wasn't convincing, and the muzzle of the gun was lowered, pointing at the floor.

It was a tense situation. Yet what happened next was so smooth and so easy. Frisk raised the revolver he was holding and fired; one shot, two shots, swiftly and easily, just like that!

The door was shut and the walls closed us in. The crash of the shots was muffled and condensed. We stared with singing ears as Manton hung in mid-air, his mouth open like he was gasping in astonishment, and his eyes bulging. Then his gun dropped from his hand and he fell backwards abruptly, fell in a sitting position. He opened his mouth, tried to say something, but a gush of blood choked his words. He reached out with his left hand as though feeling for support, and then quite suddenly fell backwards so his head banged loudly on the floor.

I got to him first. I kneeled over him, opened up his jacket. He wasn't bleeding much. I opened up his shirt, and there was one jagged hole below the centre of the breastbone and another higher up, which was close enough to have at least grazed his heart.

Manton's eyes were closed now. But his mouth kept moving like he was trying to swallow, and dribbles of fresh blood kept bubbling from the corners of his mouth. I put my fingers on the pulse in his throat. At the same time, I snapped: "Get a doctor."

Flashy-smile was right behind me. He grabbed my collar, jerked me backwards so I sprawled on the floor. "Look after this guy," he rapped.

"What the hell?" I yelled, but as I scrambled to my feet, the battered features of Jenks thrust close to mine. There was a hard, uncompromising ring of steel poking at my belly. "Easy, pal," he advised. "Back up against the wall. You don't wanna get yourself in trouble."

I backed up against the wall. Everything had happened so quickly I was bewildered. I glanced at Frisk, hoping maybe he'd be giving some orders. He was standing behind his desk, his face still white and terrified. He was staring at the gun, which he'd dropped on his desk like it was a poisonous snake.

Flashy-smile crossed swiftly to the office door. Jenks called after him, warningly: "Say, you ain't gettin' a doctor?"

Flashy-smile carefully locked the door; put the key in his pocket. He said, meaningfully: "A doctor ain't needed."

Frisk's panic-stricken eyes climbed slowly from the desk towards flashy-smile. His lips trembled. They trembled so much I could hardly hear his words. "He isn't ... isn't ... dead!"

Flashy-smile showed his teeth in a wide grin. "Sure," he said. "What d'ya expect? Two slugs in the chest are liable to kill a guy."

Frisk stood like stone for several seconds. Then he dropped into his chair, buried his face in his hands and moaned aloud: "I've killed him. I've killed him!"

I licked my lips. I didn't like any of this. The door was locked and I had the uneasy feeling I'd seen too much.

"Look, fellas," I said. "Better call the cops."

"Shuddup," snarled Jenks.

"It's your duty," I told him. "You've gotta call the cops. Nobody's gonna beef any. It was self-defence, wasn't it?"

"Not the way the cops will build it up," said flashy-smile.

"But that's the way it was," I protested. "I'll be a witness it was self-defence." I was telling myself that if I ever got outta there, I was gonna tell it just the way it was: cold-blooded murder. Although Manton had pointed a gun, it was by no means certain he was gonna use it.

Frisk lifted his head from his hands, stared at me levelly. He'd got himself under control now. "That won't be any good," he said. "The cops would try to hang it on me. Even if they couldn't hang it on me, they'd get me a stretch for manslaughter."

Flashy-smile shook his head admonishingly. "You shouldn't have done it, boss," he said. "You shouldn't have done it."

Frisk sighed. "All this time, I've kept my hands clean," he almost moaned. "They've never had anything on me. And now ... this!"

This reaction was typical of him. Not one thought for the poor devil whose life he had taken. Just selfish regret his action had got him in a jam.

Jenks said, meaningfully: "There was one guy too many who saw everything."

That was when Frisk really became aware of my presence. His eyes widened, became hunted. "That's what I mean," he said. "It's not just Manton. Now it's him." For the first time, he realized the full impact of my menace to him. His voice was scared. "Don't let him go, Jenks," he ordered. "Don't let him out of this room."

Jenks grinned easily, ground the gun barrel into my belly. "You ain't goin' anywhere?" he mocked.

Frisk said, fluttering a nervous hand: "We've gotta watch out for him. He's gonna be dangerous. I've gotta think." He muttered beneath his breath, talking to himself. "Always kept my hands clean until now. What a helluva thing to happen!"

I hadn't any wrong ideas about Frisk. He was yella all the way through. Too yella to execute his own killings. He paid other guys to do it. That's how he kept himself free from the cops.

Flashy-smile said, pointedly: "We've gotta act quick, boss. This ain't the kinda thing you can sleep on."

Frisk agreed nervously. "Yeah. We've gotta act quick." His fingers drummed on his desk. "We've gotta get the body out of here somehow. Can't have it around the place. That's what you'd better do, Gunn. Get him outta here. Drop him in a ditch somewhere."

Flashy-smile, or Gunn, as I now learnt his name to be, took out a cigarette, lit it casually. He was cool for a guy who'd had the disposal of a murdered man dumped in his lap. "I figure we can be smart, boss," he drawled. "We can fix two guys with one murder. We can get rid of Manton, and we can clear you, too!"

There was a kinda stony silence. With a flutter of apprehension, I realized all three of them were staring at me with new and sudden interest.

CHAPTER FIVE

Everything had happened so quickly – the killing of Manton and the smooth acceptance of it by Frisk's bodyguard – that I was bewildered, my mental processes dulled and not working so quickly as theirs.

As those three pairs of eyes stared at me, I stared back, uncomprehendingly. Then slowly, very slowly, I did begin to understand dimly.

"Get your hands up, bud," rasped Jenks. He jabbed with the gun barrel. Reluctantly I raised my hands. There was a queer, hollow feeling inside me. I looked at Frisk and demanded: "What's the meaning of this?"

The colour had come back to his cheeks now. He was rapidly gaining control of himself. "Better get outside, Gunn. See if anyone heard those shots."

Gunn moved swiftly and smoothly, reappeared within a few moments, locking the door behind him with a grin of satisfaction on his face. "Everything's fine," he said. "They couldn't even hear a bomb. Their own hearts are beating too loudly!"

Frisk nodded with satisfaction. Then he looked at Jenks meaningfully. I tried to analyse that silent message, but once again my thinking processes were way behind theirs. The gun barrel jabbed into my belly: this time, so mercilessly that it drove the air out of my lungs, caused me to double over in agony.

Jenks worked like a machine. My bowed head was a defenceless and perfect target. He smashed the gun butt on the nape of my neck at the base of the skull. It wasn't very painful. It kinda paralysed me with a red-hot tingling sensation. In a red haze, I realized I was lying on the floor, the room expanding and contracting and hot pins and needles jabbing me all over. There was no resistance in me when they pulled my hands behind me, lashed them securely with electric flex from the table lamp.

I wasn't very sure about anything that was happening. I could see only their blurred faces as they turned me on my back. Jenks's face loomed close as he knelt over me. He was lifting my head, holding it. I couldn't understand why he should be doing that. And by this time my thinking processes were almost at a standstill. Because there was but a split second of understanding when a blurred fist began its journey. It finished its journey somewhere inside my head amidst agonized blackness.

I don't know how long I was unconscious. When I opened my eyes, blinked around hazily, Frisk was leaning against the cocktail cabinet, smoking a cigarette through a long holder. Gunn was lifting something shiny from a small polished box. I shook my head to clear it, blinked my eyes. Gunn was quick to notice, raised his crafty eyes to mine and smiled his toothy smile. "Have a nice little kip?" he mocked.

I moved uncomfortably, felt burning pain around my wrists. I was wedged in Frisk's chair, my hands tied behind me and secured to the chair so I couldn't move. Something else was wrong, too. Jenks wasn't there!

My head was aching intolerably. I bleared towards Frisk. "What are you guys up to?" I demanded.

Frisk was completely self-composed now. He smiled, kindly and indulgently. "Need I say I regret this, Mr Martin?" He shrugged his shoulders. "Just a whim of fate. If you'd not thought to change a cheque, this would never have occurred." He shrugged his shoulders again. "As it is ... I can only offer my regrets."

My head ached so bad it made me angry. "What the hell are you talking about?" I demanded. "Just let me go, or I'll raise all hell."

He smiled tolerantly. "We shall let you go ... eventually!" The way he spoke indicated release was gonna mean a lotta grief for me. I was in some tough kinda jam. The hell of it was, I didn't know what kinda jam.

"What are you playing at?" I demanded. "What d'you reckon you can pull?"

Gunn was still toying with that box. I could see more clearly now, see what he was handling. It was a long, glittering hypodermic. He was busy charging it with transparent liquid from gelatine capsules. He paused momentarily to look at me with malicious satisfaction. "You did it wrong, fella," he mocked. "You shouldn't have put a coupla slugs in that guy." His eyes indicated Manton, who was lying the other side of the desk. I could only see his feet.

"You're crazy," I burst out. "You can't pin this on me. I saw it all." I licked my lips and told a white lie. "Frisk killed him in self-defence. There isn't a jury could hang it on him if they wanted."

Frisk chuckled. But there was no humour in his chuckle. "You don't understand," he said gently. "You killed him. There isn't the slightest question of it."

I got that fluttery feeling in my belly again. I knew false accusations wouldn't get them anywhere. Manton had been killed in Frisk's office, and a searching examination of witnesses would bring out the true facts. But, just the same, I was scared. I was scared because they were so confident.

I put a brave face on it. "That suits me fine," I said. "You can't get the cops here soon enough for me."

Frisk tut-tutted. "Why should the cops come here? Why should we be involved?"

I stared at him with startled eyes. Gunn gave a grunt of satisfaction, straightened up, holding the hypodermic firmly, thumb poised, ready to press home the plunger. He held it ominously, pointed it towards me. I stared at the long needle with its fine, penetrating point. There was a sudden dryness in my throat. "What are you gonna do?" I croaked.

"We're gonna fix you, pal," he said. It was probably his idea, and he was proud of it. He couldn't resist telling me. He gestured with the hypodermic. "You're gonna take a long nap, pal," he said. "A real long nap. You won't wake up until after the cops find you. You'll be drunk, and with a stiff in the back of your car. You'll have the murder gun in your hand smothered with your fingerprints. You'll never be smart enough to talk yourself out of that."

My head was whirling. "You won't get away ..."

There was a swift succession of raps on the door. Frisk unlocked the door, opened up for Jenks.

Frisk barked at him: "Did you get it?"

"Sure, boss. I got an old, worn-out heap. Won't attract so much attention."

"Are you sure nobody saw you?"

Jenks looked at him indignantly. "D'you think I'm nutty?"

Gunn said, grimly: "You're just in time. Give me a hand with this guy, will ya?"

I started struggling then. I almost overturned the chair. Jenks got around back of me, locked his arm around my neck, straining my head back and threatening to snap my spinal cord. His arm was across my windpipe, cutting off my breath so I could only whisper a protest.

I felt Gunn unbuttoning my vest, removing my tie and unbuttoning my shirt. Suddenly everything was so unbearably unfair and unbelievable.

For fifteen years I'd been planning revenge, waiting for my opportunity. Now, with everything prepared, there was this boomerang.

Gunn was baring my shoulder now, and I couldn't move a muscle. I felt his fingers pulling my clothing off my shoulder. Then came the hot stab of the needle, probing ever deeper so that I writhed with the agony of it. Hot, bitter shame rolled over me in a flood of despair. After all my careful planning for revenge, it was galling to have this happening to me. Find myself being framed for murder. And by Frisk, of all people!

The plunger was being forced home slowly. I could feel the colourless liquid spurting into my blood stream. It was ice-cold, numbing and rapidly spreading. As a dull leadenness began to possess my mind, I made one last, superhuman effort to break away, risking a broken neck and strangulation. With a wild, upwards heave, I tried to fling myself sideways from the chair. It caught Jenks by surprise, and I almost succeeded. The chair half-toppled on its side, and there was a burning, searing wrench in my arm. Gunn swore viciously, and Jenks applied an even stronger lock on my neck.

Gunn snarled angrily: "I told you to hold him. Look what you've done now."

"He won't move no more," promised Jenks grimly.

Frisk's cool, confident voice ordered: "Give him the rest of the jolt."

"The needle's snapped," growled Gunn.

There was a kinda paralysis overcoming me now. That cold dullness had entered my veins, was pulsing through my body, paralysing every nerve centre it encountered. It was flowing upwards towards my head, very soon would be numbing my thoughts and brain.

"How much did you give him?" asked Frisk. But his voice sounded loud and booming, as though through a long tunnel.

"Half a jolt," said Gunn. He added, thoughtfully: "Maybe it's better that way. Too much might make the cops suspicious."

Jenks let my head go. I had lost control of it. My chin flopped forward on my chest. With a tremendous effort of will-power, I was able to raise my eyes. They were all three standing and watching me solemnly.

"How long does it take?" asked Frisk.

"Just a moment now," said Gunn. "Takes a little time to work around to the brain. It'll be any moment now."

He was right. I never knew when it happened. It was like going to sleep when you didn't know you were going to sleep.

CHAPTER SIX

It was like waking after a tremendous binge the night before. Only ten times more so. I musta been hunched with my arms on the steering wheel and my eyes open for maybe half-an-hour or more without realizing I was conscious.

Then, very dimly, I became aware I was sitting in a car, cold and dazed and enveloped in the smell of raw whisky. My mind was sluggish, operating like a car with the hand-brake on. I knew it was sluggish, but couldn't make it work any faster.

Little by little, I snatched at pieces of understanding, fitted them together. I was in a car. I was out in the country and dawn was just breaking. My head ached intolerably, my wrists and arms were painful and my mouth was full of cotton wool. Also, I was enveloped in the stink of whisky. My clothes were soaked in it. There was an empty bottle lying on the seat beside me. I stared at it a long while. None of this made any sense.

I couldn't understand why I was here, who I was or where I had been going. I tried to spit the cotton wool from my mouth, found it was my tongue I was trying to spit out. Suddenly I wanted a drink. I wanted it awfully badly. I opened the door of the car, climbed outside. All my movements were weak and unreal.

The sharp morning air did something for me. I stood beside the car, leaning on the front wing and gulping at it. I drew in deep breaths, exhaled until my lungs were empty. It was like drawing in fresh, life-giving air and breathing out sour, tainted fumes. I breathed deeply that way for maybe ten minutes, feeling stronger and stronger every minute. Then, from far away, I heard the loud roar of a high-powered car, heard it before I could see it. A speeding flash of ivory swooping out of sight and then reappearing on the crest of the next hill.

I watched it approaching, wondered about it. I took my hand off the front wing and walked a couple of paces, was surprised to find I was swaying. I stepped back, fumbled for the wing to support myself. The car swept towards me. I watched it with screwed up eyes, feeling stupefied and vaguely wondering if I could get a drink of water.

It roared towards me, speeding like some avenging monster. Then it was swerving into the side of the road, tyres squealing protestingly as brakes were applied. It jolted to a halt just opposite me, a long, ivory-cream coupe that musta cost a fortune.

The door swung open and the driver clambered out. She was a dame dressed in a blood-red frock, her blonde, wind-swept hair attractively dishevelled. She clip-clopped across the road on high-heeled shoes, peered at me with anxious eyes. "Are you all right?" she asked.

I worked up a grin. "I'll be all right in a minute," I croaked. I brushed my hair back off my forehead, swayed once again. Instinctively helpful, she stepped close, took my arm. Then her nose crinkled and her attitude changed. "I wouldn't do any more driving if I were you," she said severely. "You'd better sleep it off."

Her eyes were cool and blue. They were staring at me like she was willing me to obey her. I liked her looking at me like that. It helped to steady me. I was remembering other things now, little disjointed things. A flashy-smile guy named Gunn and a hard-faced night-club cashier. There was something else too, something really important. I couldn't figure it out right then.

"I wanna drink," I managed to say. I tried to moisten my dry mouth. "I wanna drink," I repeated.

"Just you take it easy," she advised. "You've had too much to drink already."

I reached down into my mind, came up with an idea. "No," I said vaguely. "That's not it. Not too much to drink. There's something else."

"You've got yourself a skinful," she said. "Just sit down and sleep it off. You'll feel better afterwards."

I was suddenly afraid she would leave me. "No, don't go," I said urgently. And there were other things in my mind now;

dark, ugly things, fleeting impressions that eluded me. I fought hard to clutch them, hold them still so I could examine them.

"You do as I say," she said firmly. "You get back in your car, sit there and sleep it off." Even as she was talking, she was urging me towards the door, opening the door for me.

She saw it the same time as I did. It was on the car-floor, squat and ugly. Her fingers tensed on my arm. "Say! That thing's not loaded, is it?" she asked.

I stared at it. It was coming to me now. Manton and Frisk. The hypodermic! It was a dream, a wild fantastic dream. But it was true. The gun was there, just like they said it would be.

Seeing it was like a cold water douche. Suddenly everything became clear like a shutter had lifted in my mind and I could remember everything that had happened. There was the whisky bottle on the seat – empty! I stunk of whisky, and the incriminating revolver was on the floor. I'd had only a small jolt from that hypodermic. I'd come around sooner than they expected, recovered consciousness before curious cops pulled into the side of the road to investigate why a man was slumped over the wheel of a stationary car.

I knew it all in a flash. Realized this dame herself could be a witness against me. I pulled away from her. "Forget it, sister," I said harshly. "Scram, will ya?"

She tugged at my arm. "You're high," she said contemptuously. "Get inside off the road, where you won't be knocked down. And don't start playing with that gun or you'll ..." Her voice broke off.

There was sudden, hard tenseness inside her that I sensed immediately. I followed the direction of her eyes. She was staring into the back of the car. I could see it the same as she could. It was Manton right enough, lying there on the floor of the car, doubled up strangely and with the kinda motionlessness that told you right away he was dead.

She gaped, her blue eyes filled with horror. She let go my arm, backed a coupla paces, like she was being approached by a poisonous snake. Then her eyes flicked to mine, filled with terror. She spun around, began running madly towards her coupe.

She didn't leave me much time for thinking. That look of terror in her eyes showed she'd jumped to the obvious conclusion, believed I'd killed him. She wanted to get away as quick as she knew how. And the first telephone she came to, she'd have the cops sealing off the district, rounding up all suspects. Rounding up *me*!

I acted instinctively. I was in a jam, a real tough jam. If I was gonna get myself outta that jam, I had to have time. I just had to stop that dame giving the alarm. I went after her, reached her just as she swung open the door of her car. I grabbed her wrists, pulled her back into the road.

"Now listen to me," I said. "I can explain all this. If you'll only ..."

There was no mistaking the terror in her eyes. She was frantic to get away from me, burying small, even teeth in my wrist, wresting herself free as I grunted with the sudden sharp pain of it. Then she was running down the centre of the road, like her life depended on it.

It was the blind instinct to survive that motivated me then. I just had to have time. Once in the hands of the cops, I wouldn't have a chance. I went after her, my shoes pounding heavily on the gravel behind her.

Though she was scared, she musta been using her head, figuring the right moves at the right time. At the last moment, as I was reaching to grasp her shoulder, she shot me a swift, terrified glance, twisted unexpectedly, dodged beneath my outstretched arm and thrust her foot between my legs so that I staggered, sprawled on hands and knees.

It was sheer terror that gave her strength. By the time I'd scrambled to my feet, she was half way back to her car, her feet barely touching the ground. I went after her, ran like I'd never run before. If she hadn't been so panic-stricken and had remembered to turn on the engine, she'd lave got away. As it was, she was thumbing the starter hopelessly for the third time when I reached her.

I pulled open the door. Like an eel, she slipped to the other side, evading my outstretched hands. I made another grab for her, but the gear lever got in my way. She scrambled over the seat into the back of the car.

She wasn't an easy dame to reason with. And I just had to keep her quiet. I launched myself over the back seat and fell, dragging her down with me. She squealed loudly, clawed my hands with sharp fingernails, kicked with murderously sharp heels, and somehow scrambled to her feet.

In that moment, on the early morning air, I heard the sound of another car approaching. That got me really scared. I pictured other folk arriving on the scene, the girl's hysterical account of how I was assaulting her. I forgot all scruples then. I grabbed her legs, jerked hard so she sprawled on top of me. Now I was really manhandling her. This was no time for half-measures. I wrestled her around until she was lying face downwards. I twisted her arms up behind her back and put on a lock she was powerless to move. I spread-eagled myself across her, rammed her nose and mouth hard against the carpet so she couldn't scream. I held her that way with my heart in my mouth until the roar of the passing car diminished a distant hum.

Now I was in trouble. Real trouble. The dame wasn't easy to reason with in the first place. With every passing minute, more and more traffic would be on the roads. Now I had to figure up some way of keeping the dame quiet until I could get clear from the district.

But how to keep the dame quiet?

Then I got it. At first it was so fantastic I almost rejected it. But it was the only sure way. I let her lift her head to draw a few breaths while I told her what I intended to do. But she took only one breath. Then she began screaming her lungs out.

I couldn't reason with her. I'd have to do it and explain why later.

That gave me another problem. It was a cinch she wasn't going with me willingly. I shrugged my shoulders. In that case, she'd have to go whether she liked it or not.

Lying on her belly the way she was, with her arms doubled up behind her, she couldn't give me much of an argument. I put on the pressure, forced her arms even higher until bones creaked and she screeched with the pain of it. I kept her hands in that position, held them with one hand. Pain strained her body to rigidity. Her slightest movement made the pain unbearable. She was tense and rigid, grinding her teeth with the agony of it. I used the handiest thing for binding her wrists. She was already terrified of me. It wasn't difficult to guess what more she was afraid of when I fumbled and unclipped her suspenders. Her sobs of pain became dull protests of tortured apprehension. But with her arms firmly held in an agonising wrestler's lock, she was unable to resist as I fingered the stocking top, rolled it down a warm, slim leg.

I hated to treat the dame this way. But I was in a serious jam. I held her arms firmly while I lashed her wrists together. I looped the free end of the stocking around her throat, tied it securely. She wasn't very happy. Her arms were strained upwards in a painful position, and every time she tried to lower them, it almost choked her.

That shoulda been enough to keep her quiet. I rolled my weight off her, said considerately: "I'd like to explain about this. You see ..."

She had plenty of grit. Although her arms were tied in that painful position, she hacked upwards with her foot, the one still shod. The sharp heel gouged into my shin.

What could be done with a dame like that? She just had to be tied down. I grabbed her ankle as the vicious heel jagged towards me again, pulled off her shoe. The bare heel of her other foot nearly pulped my nose. She wasn't giving me any alternative. The first stocking had been relatively easy to remove. Now she was squirming, twisting and shrieking all the time. I had to clamp her kicking legs under my arm while I fumbled to strip off her other stocking. She acted like I was taking her for a ride and this was her last chance to keep alive. I was sweating by the time I managed to lash her ankles together. I eased up then. But she didn't. As soon as I released her, she kinda rolled over, somehow struggled to her knees.

That was the final straw. I pushed her down, doubled her legs behind her, used my tie to draw her ankles towards her bound wrists. That did quieten her! When she tried to straighten out, her ankles pulled on her wrists and her wrists pulled on her throat, threatening to choke her. She learned quickly. She only tried straightening out once.

But she still had lungs and still had a mouth. She used them both. She was a dame who never knew when it was smart to stop resisting. I used my handkerchief to gag her, and nearly lost the top of my finger doing it. I had to seize her hair, strain her head back until her neck almost cracked, before she let up. My pain was so intense, I barely restrained myself from punching her.

That dame sure caused me trouble. It took ten minutes or more to fasten her that way. I spread-eagled myself over her while another car flashed by, and then reached over to the driving seat for a gaily-coloured travelling blanket. It covered her completely. I checked to make sure no other cars were approaching, crossed the road to the car that contained Manton. I took the empty whisky bottle, slung it in the bushes. I picked up the revolver carefully with my handkerchief, scrupulously cleaned off all fingerprints and, with a shudder of revulsion, pressed Manton's cold stiff fingers around the butt. It wasn't likely the cops would believe Manton committed suicide. But it would give them something to think about.

I went back to the coupe, climbed in behind the steering wheel. It was a beautiful job, musta cost a small fortune. I glanced over the seat at the gaily-coloured blanket behind me. It moved just slightly. "Sorry, lady," I apologised aloud. "But you just wouldn't let me do it any other way."

CHAPTER SEVEN

I was on the highroad, ten miles from Clevedon. I drove back towards town, bypassed it and drove on to my recently rented house. It was still so early, I didn't pass anyone within five miles of my place. I drove up to the front door, nailed the car at the steps and opened up the front door. I went back to the car, pulled back the blanket and saw she'd managed to squirm around so she was lying on her back. I saw more than that. Her eyes were closed and her face was blue.

It scared me. I'd never seen anyone that blue before. I ripped open the car door, tore the gag from her mouth. Her tongue lolled out. That got me worried even worse. I released the stocking that was cutting into her windpipe and carried her into the house. Only my room was furnished, so I took her there, laid her on the bed and released her wrists and ankles.

Her face was still blue. She didn't seem to be breathing. I opened her bodice, pulled her underclothing to one side and pressed my ear to her heart. I could detect a faint beating. I was so worried, my hands were shaking. I got brandy, forced it between her lips a spoonful at a time. Then I turned her on her belly, began to bear down on her the way you do on folk who are almost drowned.

I've never felt so relieved as when I saw a red flush begin to replace the bluish tinge of her cheeks. But her eyes didn't open for a full twenty minutes after that.

First she stared at me dazedly, uncomprehendingly. Then, a few moments later, fear sprang into her eyes, and she screamed, rolled across the bed to the opposite side from me, made a wild dash towards the door. I caught her around the waist, lifted her off the floor. "If you'll only just listen to me ..." I began.

She wasn't willing to listen to anything or anybody. She was screaming madly, flailing at me with bare feet and sharp fingernails. Fear gave her new strength. She twisted away from me, put the bed between us, shrieked frantically: "Don't touch me. Don't dare touch me."

Her dress was unbuttoned at the front and her underclothing disarranged. She'd figured she had plenty of reason to keep away from me.

"You don't understand," I began. "There's a perfectly reasonable ..."

She picked up a light chair, swung it above her head. Her eyes were panic-stricken. "Keep away," she warned fiercely. "Keep away from me."

"If you'll only just listen ..." I began. I took a coupla paces towards her. She hurled the chair at me. I saw it coming all the way, went in underneath it and caught her around the waist.

I couldn't do a thing with her until she'd cooled down and was ready to listen to reason. She fought every inch of the way as I wrestled her out of my room, along the corridor and into another room. That room was completely bare. I thrust her inside, turned the key in the lock and listened to her hammering the panels, screaming to be let out.

I sighed wearily. After all that had happened, I was exhausted. Yet there was still so much to do. I went downstairs, drove her car around back into the garage. It was a big garage. I pulled my car across in front of hers, in case anyone with big eyes should happen to be around.

When I got upstairs, she'd quit pounding the door. That was all to the good. Give her an hour to cool off, and she'd listen to facts.

But what were the facts? There was no point in evading the issue. The main fact was, I was out to get Frisk. More than that, I had to duck out from under this murder rap he'd swung on me. All ways, it added up to one thing. That dame was gonna have to stick around until I'd fixed everything and was ready to melt away into the obscurity of America, assuming my own real name in that distant part of the States where I'd lived for most of the past fifteen years.

Yeah, the girl had to stick around. And although I hadn't known her long, I was sure of one thing. She wasn't gonna stick around without persuasion.

Where was she going to stay? She was a dame, and it wasn't her fault she was gonna be my guest. I had to make her comfortable. She would have to have my room, the only furnished room in the house.

I wanted more than anything else to sit back and take a rest. But this job was urgent. I went downstairs, got my tool box and a length of fine but strong chain.

I measured off ten feet of chain, allowing a couple of feet aound her waist and eight feet of slack. I chose the position for it carefully, firmly screwed a hasp into the door-frame of the bathroom door. It prevented the door from closing. I attached one end of the chain to the hasp with a strong padlock and looped the other end around my own waist, tested it. The chain allowed me enough movement to wash in the bathroom but not to reach the window. Then I tested in the other direction, and realized I'd have to move the bed nearer. All other moveable articles that could be thrown or used as offensive weapons, I shifted beyond range of the chain.

All I had to do now was fasten the chain tightly around her waist and padlock it. She'd have freedom of movement and relative comfort, be able to shower when she wanted and sleep comfortably in bed. It was gonna be tough on her. But it was liable to be much tougher on me if I didn't do this. I went into the corridor and along to the other door, unlocked it. One swift glance told me everything. I ran to the open window, stared down. She'd taken off her red dress, ripped it into lengths and tied them together. One end of the home-made rope was tied to the window-blind catch. She was half-way down, lowering herself carefully, levering the soles of her bare feet against the wall.

It was a crazy thing to do. That dress fabric was woven, liable to snap beneath her weight.

I ran down the stairs, burst out of the house and ran around back. I reached her just as she reached ground. She actually lowered herself into my arms. And having got so near to freedom, she was even more desperate to escape. She fought me furiously, biting, scratching and kicking. Once again I acted ungentlemanly, twisted her arms painfully, herded her in front of me, she whimpering with pain and resisting every step of the way.

She made me feel a heel. I didn't wanna treat her that way. But I had no alternative. And she was in her underclothes now; brief, scanty underclothing that meant all the time I was grappling with her, I was handling bare flesh. She made me feel worse by resisting, like I was mauling her deliberately.

She struggled every inch of the way, threw her weight backwards on me as I forced her up the stairs, twisted and writhed like she had the strength of ten dames. When I got her into my room and forced her towards the bed, her resistance doubled. She was quite sure now what I had in mind. She made me put pressure on her arms, which I hated, knowing I was hurting her cruelly. She made a superhuman effort when we reached the bed, one final attempt to squirm away. I exerted my strength, lifted her from her feet, threw her on the bed, face down. She was expecting other things. That maybe was why she didn't resist when I looped the chain around her waist, pulled it tight and sealed it with a padlock.

I got up, sweating, and backed away from her, wiped my arm across my forehead. She lay there for a moment as though surprised by being so suddenly released. Then she sat up quickly, turned around to face me. There was apprehension, fear and just a hint of surprise in her eyes. In the same moment, she clutched at the broken strap of her cami-knickers, held her bodice so it covered her bare breast. Her other hand went to her waist, fingers fumbled at the chain. She looked down at it, shocked, scrambled off the bed, and suddenly realized she was tethered like a dog in a kennel. Her hunted eyes found mine. The apprehension in those blue eyes was deep and bitter. She backed until she was pressed up tight against the wall. She was scared. No matter how much she struggled now, she could not escape me.

This was my first let-up since I'd met her. I didn't have to worry about her any more. She'd never get off that chain, except with a hacksaw or padlock key. For the first time, I was able to look at her and see her as a woman instead of a threat to my liberty. I liked what I saw. She was attractive, with long, slim legs; a compact, beautifully-proportioned body and the kinda figure that makes guys turn to look a second time. I was seeing her to the best advantage, because all she'd been wearing under that red dress was black cami-knickers; black-lace cami-knickers through which the milky white of her skin gleamed invitingly. She wore one other article of clothing. A slender suspender girdle. She wore it beneath the cami-knickers. I could see it because the lace-work was so fine, so delicate and so revealing.

Her face was white, she was breathing heavily and she was using both hands to tie the broken shoulder strap. She was still pressed against the wall as far from me as she could get. The hunted expression in her eyes showed she expected me to spring at any moment.

"I just want to explain ..." I began.

She snarled, baring her teeth like a tigress at bay. "Murderer," she spat at me. "Murderer!"

She was a sweet-looking dame. It hurt me to see the blazing contempt in her eyes. I'd been through so much already. Now I was feeling so exhausted, I hadn't the strength to argue or even explain.

"So I'm a murderer," I agreed wearily. "Being in for one killing or two makes little difference. I only hang once." I pointed my finger at her. "What's to stop me bumping you right now?"

Suddenly she wasn't scared any more. She stared at me, pressed herself back against the wall, but the fear had left her eyes. She kinda sucked in her breath. "Yeah," she taunted. "That's what I'd like to know. What's to stop you killing me now?"

I said ominously: "Bear it in mind. Keep thinking about it. And keep quiet for a coupla hours, or maybe I'll slit your throat."

Maybe I said it with conviction. As I spoke, her hands went up to her throat, encircled it protectively,

"That's the idea, honey," I gritted. "You keep good and scared and pipe down for a coupla hours." I turned away from her, stumbled across to the other side of the room, sank wearily into a deep, comfortable armchair. I stretched out luxuriously, sighed with contentment. She was watching me curiously. After a moment, she asked anxiously: "What are you going to do?"

I yawned. "Get some sleep," I said. I yawned again. "A coupla hours sleep. That's what I need."

"I mean ... what are you going to do about me?"

I worked a grim note into my voice, stared at her with hard eyes. "Cut your throat maybe if you don't pipe down."

She shut up, still stood there, watching me. After a time, my eyelids began to flutter. I musta dozed for a few minutes. When I opened my eyes a little later, she was curled up on the bed, crouched there with her cheeks resting on her hands. She was staring at me like I was some laboratory subject she was analysing.

Maybe it was the unusual exertion, maybe it was the after-effects of that drug, or maybe it was the whisky Gunn had forced between my lips, while I lay unconscious. I couldn't keep my eyes open any longer. My eyelids inexorably closed, and I slept.

CHAPTER EIGHT

I musta slept for two or three hours. I awoke with a start, tensed because I knew I was in trouble.

My eyes turned towards the dame, and the next moment I was climbing out of my chair in desperate anxiety. The bathroom door was closed as far as the chain would permit. I almost thrust it open and burst into the bathroom. I stopped myself just in time.

"Hey. Are you in there?" I demanded.

There was a moment's silence. Then she said, quietly and wearily: "Go away. Leave me alone."

"How long have you been in there?"

"I've only just ..."

"If you're not out in three minutes, I'm coming in," I warned.

"Why you ..." she choked with indignation.

I paced up and down the room, lit a cigarette. "All right," I called. "Three minutes up. I'm coming in."

"I'm coming," she answered breathlessly. The door opened and she sidled out. There was an angry flush on her cheeks and her eyes glinted with annoyance. I looked her over, slowly and scrutinizingly. The chain was still firmly secured around her waist. That was reassuring. Just for a moment, I'd been scared she'd managed to work that chain down over her hips. I could see now it was drawn too tightly for that.

She climbed on the bed, pulled a sheet up around her. "Don't keep looking at me like that!" she flared.

"Stripping your dress was your idea," I told her.

She flushed even more. "Haven't you anything I can wear?"

"Getting squeamish kinda sudden?"

She sat and glared at me. There was still a hint of fear deep down in her eyes. But she'd had time to cool off, adjust herself to her circumstances.

I got busy making coffee. My upper arm was painful where I'd been jabbed with that hypodermic. I noticed it more and more as I sliced bacon, dropped it into sizzling fat. It was a long while since I'd eaten. An appetising aroma filled the air, sharpened my appetite.

I put a large cup of coffee, bacon and bread on a tray. I knew just how far that chain would allow her to move. I'd formed in my mind's eye a mental boundary line over which I shouldn't pass if I didn't want to tangle with her. I kept my side of the boundary line, pushed the tray over into her territory. "Get this inside you," I told her. She tossed her head, sniffed disdainfully. "I don't eat with murderers!"

I shrugged my shoulders disinterestedly. "Suits me."

I didn't realise I was so hungry. I ate slowly and with relish. Meanwhile, she sat on the bed, curled up with the sheet around her, watching me with evident disapproval. The aroma of that coffee was lingering in the air. It proved more than she could resist. After a little while, she reluctantly sidled off the bed, approached the tray, inspected it critically. I ignored her. She picked up the tray, carried it back to the bed, sat there drinking the coffee. A little later she started on the bacon.

She was only halfway through by the time I'd finished. I leaned back in my chair with satisfaction, lit a cigarette and looked at her directly for the first time since she'd started eating. "Tastes good, doesn't it?"

She glared at me. "What am I supposed to do? Say thank you?"

"I don't *have* to feed you," I pointed out.

She tossed her head, sniffed contemptuously. But she didn't stop eating. When she was through, she pushed the tray on one side, stared at me hostilely.

"Cigarette?" I invited.

"Do I have to go on my knees for it?"

I took a new pack from my pocket, tossed it to her. She caught it neatly. I was gonna throw her a box of matches, then hesitated. A dame like her could raise all hell with matches, setting the bedclothes alight, burning the place down in a desperate effort to get away. My own cigarette was almost finished. I put it in a saucer, edged it across the boundary line. "Help yourself to a light."

She was furious. She figured I did that so she would have to come out from under the sheets. At the same time, she wanted that smoke badly. She came over and got her light, eyes flashing angrily all the time. And because she was so self-conscious, I noticed her. Noticed her as a woman, I mean. Noticed how her skin gleamed through her undergarment, the contrast between the silky blackness of the suspender tags against the milky-white of her thighs and the deep cleavage between her breasts as she stooped.

Conscious of my scrutiny, she scuttled back to the bed, pulled the sheet around her before she lit the cigarette. She held my dog-end between her fingers like the part my lips had touched was leprous. She glanced around, wondering where to put the dog-end, and then got a better idea. She threw it at me.

It fell short. I grinned amiably, kicked it off the carpet and ground it beneath my heel on the wooden skirting board.

I took a chair, pulled it almost to the boundary line and sat facing her comfortably. "What's your name?" I asked conversationally.

"As if you don't know," she sneered.

"Okay," I said. "You don't have to be sociable. But I owe you an explanation. I owe you an apology, too."

"Now fancy that," she mocked.

I looked at her levelly. "I didn't kill that guy," I said.

"He wasn't even dead," she mocked. "You don't know a thing about it. You weren't even there when it happened. And I'm not chained up like a dog."

"I can understand you not believing me," I said wearily. "I was framed. I recovered consciousness sooner than expected. You jumped to the wrong conclusion the same way as the cops would have done."

"Save it for the judge," she sneered.

I breathed hard. "You're not an easy dame to get along with."

"You aren't exactly a helpful playmate yourself," she retorted.

I felt in my pocket for another cigarette, flinched as red hot pain stabbed in my upper arm. That needle sure had made me sore. "I'm sorry about you," I said sincerely. "It was just your bad luck you happened along. I've gotta straighten this thing out, get myself in the clear. I won't have a chance if you go squawking to the cops." I sighed. "You see the way it is. I've just gotta stop you squawking."

She sneered. "Yeah, that's all. You just wanna stop me squawking. That's why you've got this set-up, everything laid on to keep me a prisoner."

I stared at her. "You talk like I'd planned all this. You're not getting the crazy idea I like doing this?"

"Cut out the frills," she said crudely. "I know why I'm here. So do you. It's a dangerous game to play, and you'll never get away with it. It may take a year, it may take a coupla years. But they'll get you, brother." Her eyes flashed, and her breasts heaved. "And I hope they'll hang you!" she finished.

I could understand the dame being sore. But she talked like I had some personal kinda motive for treating her this way. "I don't know how long you're gonna be here," I said. "Not too long, I hope. You can fight back at me all the time you're here. Or you can accept the way things are. It'll make it easier for you and for me if you accept everything quietly."

She tossed her head, and the movement caused the long chain to clink. "Make myself comfortable!" she said in disgust.

"I'll tell you just once more," I said levelly. "I didn't kill that guy. I was framed."

"Stop it," she drawled. "You make me weep."

"Now tell me about yourself," I said. "What's your name? Who are your folks? Can I get in touch with them, make some excuse to explain your absence?"

"Perhaps you'd like me to write them a letter?"

"Yeah," I said. "That's a good idea. You write them a letter. If it's okay, I'll see they get it."

Her cheeks blazed with anger. She swung herself off the bed, pushed through into the bathroom, shut the door behind her as far as she was able.

She showed pretty clearly she wasn't gonna do any more talking. I got up, winced with a sudden hot stab of pain in my arm, and made my way to one of the other rooms, where I could take a shower. There was an ugly red swelling on my arm where that hypodermic needle had jabbed. I felt the spot tenderly, and pain burned deep down inside my arm. The flesh was swollen and reddened. As a doctor, Gunn would have made a good butcher.

I was fresher when I was through washing. I went back to my room, and the dame was still in the bathroom. She musta been in there half an hour. It worried me. All the time she was in there, I couldn't see what she was doing. I was worried she might figure out some way to get loose. I called out to her. She didn't reply. I called out again, crossed over to the bathroom door. She still didn't reply.

I pushed at the bathroom door, rapped on the panels. It resisted me. "Listen," I gritted in a warning voice. "If you don't answer up or come out, I'm coming in. Understand?"

I got results then. A low kinda moan. The door resisted me like her weight was lying on the floor, stopping the door from opening.

I got anxious. I knuckled the panels some more. "Are you all right?" I asked loudly. "I'm coming in."

Silence.

I put my shoulder against the door, pushed. It resisted me. I pushed harder, felt the door give, got it wide enough to thrust my head around the door.

She had it all worked out. She was standing right behind the door, the slack of the chain formed into a noose. I fed my head right into it. As my head came around the door, the loop of chain was around my neck and she was straining backwards, throwing her full weight on the chain so it bit deep into my neck, cut into my windpipe, choking me with hard, metallic agony.

In a moment like that, you're panic stricken. All air is cut off, and all you can do is claw at your throat trying to loosen the killing constriction. For maybe half a minute, I was half-crazy, futilely trying to dig my fingers underneath the ring of steel that was sinking deeper and deeper into my neck. I knew I was gonna die; there was a red haze enveloping me and my heart was pounding louder and louder, echoing like a booming drum from one side of my head to the other.

She almost did for me. Another minute and I'd have been unconscious. But through the panic and fear of death, a tiny gleam of intelligence penetrated my mind. Fighting every natural primitive urge to tear that constricting ring from around my neck, a slender flash of commonsense showed what I must do.

My fingers left my throat. Just momentarily, the steel ring gouged even deeper. My hands extended on either side, grasped at the chain. Then I pulled my hands together, so that the loop of chain slackened.

It wasn't easy to do that, not while I was half-choked and gasping for breath. To counteract my move, the dame was jerking savagely on the chain, repeatedly throwing her full weight on it so the chain almost ripped through my fingers.

But the first easing of the chain destroyed my panic. I sucked air into my lungs, contented myself merely with resisting her attempts to jerk the chain from my grip. Then, as the red haze began to clear from my eyes, I exerted my strength, pulled on the chain, until slowly but inexorably she was drawn close to me. I got my arm around her waist, held her tightly while I withdrew my head from the loop. She didn't waste time. Her fingernails took strips of skin off my neck and her teeth fastened in my cheek, bit deep until I was maddened and grunting aloud with the agony of it.

The pain was unendurable. When you're suffering that kinda pain, you don't stop to think. I grabbed her hair, tugged with all my strength. Her mouth opened to squeal as she arched backwards. I didn't let up, threw my weight on her hair like I wanted to yank it out. She was squealing, arching over backwards and dropping to her knees, hands clutching at her hair to ease the pain, as a few moments earlier my own fingers had scrabbled at the chain around my neck.

My throat was crushed and lacerated. I wasn't sure I was ever gonna talk again. Blood was trickling down my cheek from the wound inflicted by her sharp teeth, and there was that burning pain in my upper arm. All those things added up. I maintained the pressure on her hair for maybe half a minute, getting a savage kinda satisfaction from her agony.

"Maybe that'll teach you," I growled grimly, when I let her go.

Her eyes were filled with tears, face twisted in pain. Her fingers massaged her scalp. She let loose a coupla sobs.

I caressed my neck tenderly. There was a ring of fire around it. "Cut out the snivelling," I snarled. "You got off light."

She was letting loose throaty sobs as she scrambled to her feet. I'd had enough. I figured she'd had enough. That was a mistake. She still had plenty of fight left in her. I didn't notice when she gathered up the slackness of chain. A length of swinging chain can be a nasty weapon.

She tried to slash me across the face with it. There wasn't enough slack to enable her to slash that high. Instead it cut across my arm, biting into my shoulder.

I was tenderly massaging my neck, quite unprepared for it. The sharp agony caused me instinctively to whirl and dive at her. She slashed again, but I caught her wrist so the chain slapped without force against my chest. "Why you little ..." I growled, as with a swift twisting jerk she got free from me, eluded my clutching arms.

She couldn't get far from me. I reached her as the chain, taut and vibrating, brought her up with a jerk. She spun around, taloned fingers swooped at my eyes. Defensively I grabbed her wrists, and then we were falling, sprawling across the bed with my fingers locked around her wrists, holding those sharp rending nails from my eyes.

Instinctively, I used my weight to clamp her down, spread-eagled myself so she couldn't move, leaned my weight on her wrists, so her shoulders were pressed against the sheets. All the time, she was struggling and writhing, spitting and snarling. But she was at a disadvantage. Her strength was no match for mine, now my weight was crushing the breath from her. Her struggles became weaker and, quite abruptly, ceased altogether.

There were long seconds while we both lay still, listening to the beatings of our hearts. I'd been hurt and I was angry. She was angry, too. Her eyes were flaming into mine, hostile and defiant. Yet my pulse was quickening, my body appreciating her nearness, the soft solidity of her body beneath mine and the quick rise and fall of her breasts as she drew breath.

"Let me go," she said fiercely. "Let me go."

I was aware of something else, too. That shoulder-strap had broken again, and one milk-white, naked breast was bewilderingly close to me.

"Let me go," she panted desperately, and the strengthless movement of her body made me acutely conscious of only a handful of flimsy underwear between us.

"You asked for it," I told her grimly. My weight still imprisoned her, my fingers maintained their firm grip around her wrists. But she wasn't struggling any longer. Her eyes were angry and defiant.

"Let me go, you swine," she burst out fiercely. Then, understanding the way I was looking at her, she made an effort, raised her head so she could stare down at herself. That was when she realized the shoulder-strap had broken again. There was nothing she could do about it. Her head fell back again like she was exhausted. She said, bitterly: "You beast. You absolute beast. Why don't you let me go?"

"Gonna promise to be good?" I demanded. I hadn't started this, but now it had happened, I was getting ideas about this dame. I liked holding her down that way, thrilled at the touch of her, found my eyes repeatedly drawn to that exposed breast, drinking in the rounded, firm perfection of it, its nearness exciting me strangely. "Gonna quit struggling?" I demanded, and knew I was playing for time, knew I was savouring every moment and that my question was unnecessary. She'd exhausted herself.

There was a pucker of annoyance to her forehead. She was still breathless, her lips parted as she panted. Her chest was heaving jerkily. Her voice and tone changed.

"Leave me alone," she pleaded. "You're crushing me."

I stared into her blue eyes. They were fearless and contemptuous.

"You gonna be good?" I asked unnecessarily, still playing for time, and my eyes slipped down from her face, down towards that other attraction that was so disturbingly close.

"Anything you say. Just leave me alone."

I looked into her eyes again. "You promise you won't start anything if I release you?" I asked. I noticed her lips were ripe and red. I noticed other things, too, in that moment. I was breathing more quickly than I should have been, there was a kinda haziness floating at the back of my mind, and she was close – so desirably close!

The pucker in her forehead became a frown of pain. "Please," she panted. "Let me go."

Her eyes were staring into mine. My face was close to hers. I forgot everything, forgot she thought me a murderer, that I'd made her my prisoner; forgot everything except her being so close to me. "I'll let you go," I said thickly. I added, meaningfully: "In just a minute."

Her eyes were staring defiantly and contemptuously into mine as I lowered my lips towards hers. At the last minute, she swiftly twisted her head on one side, arched her head up and away from me.

The chances were she would have bitten me anyway, and the roundness of her body was close to mine, fascinating, milk-white magnetism, wholly irresistible.

There was a red haze at the back of my brain, a heady rush of blood goading me on, the smell of her in my nostrils and a forgetfulness of everything except this one thing.

I kissed her.

I kissed her deliberately, caressingly and tenderly.

Instantaneous reaction seared through her at the touch. Her arms, thighs and body were instantaneously rigid, muscles drawn taut in a glorious moment that lasted a lifetime.

My lips burned, my emotions fused, soared to tremendous heights and hovered, drawn out into a slender tightrope of ecstasy that was taut, vibrating and as rigid as her body against mine.

Time had no meaning. Everything was oneness in a single moment of happiness. Rigidity strained to snapping point, ungovernable emotions captured and trembling on my lips, held there on the pinnacle of ecstasy, enduring unbearable delight until the very last moment. The touch of her, the smell of her skin, and the closeness of her! Infinite pleasure stretched with the rigidity of her body. Time had no meaning.

She relaxed suddenly as though a main spring inside her had been wound too far and had suddenly snapped, releasing in that moment all her tautened nerves and sinews so she was soft and boneless.

It lasted but a moment. She became possessed of a tremendous strength, fierce, angry strength that was bewildering in its completeness and unexpectedness. Her desperate wrists twisted from my hands, and the muscle of her body hardened and tautened, thrusting upwards at me with savage determination so I found myself rolling sideways, clutching desperately at the bed to save myself from falling.

It was a return to reality with startling, cold abruptness. I was between her and the bathroom. The chain around her waist was stretched taut and rigid as she knelt on the bed as far from me as she could get. Her eyes were strange and watchful, as though calculating my next move. But questioning, too, as though there was something she didn't understand.

I brushed my hand across my forehead, stared at her levelly, and was surprised to find I was trembling. I hadn't intended anything like that should happen. But it had happened! I wanted her to know it was just that something came over me and ...

"If you feel ..." I began.

"Get away from me," she spat. "Get away from me, you beast."

There was something strange and enigmatic about her eyes. She was angry with me. She had a right to be. But her eyes weren't all that angry.

"Get away from me. Don't dare come near me!"

I was still hot and trembly. I did what she asked, crossed to my side of that invisible boundary line. She moved too. She curled herself up on the bed, still watching me with that same enigmatic expression in her eyes. She'd cupped her truant breast, was holding it gently with both hands like she would hold a live bird, not firmly enough to hurt it but not so loosely it could fly away. I found I was noticing all kinds of things I hadn't noticed before; the gentle curve of her thighs as she sat with legs doubled up, the brevity of her cami-knickers, wide-legged so she showed her thighs almost to the hips.

She'd calmed now I was at a distance. She asked intensely: "Why did you do that?"

"Just for the record," I told her hoarsely, "I hadn't planned anything like that. It just kinda happened."

"Don't dare come near me again," she said. But her voice lacked conviction. She was still cupping that breast with both hands like it was a piece of birthday cake she wanted to carry home carefully and show everyone.

"Just don't try anything smart again," I retorted grimly. "If you try that again, I'll weigh you down with chains so you can't even move."

"Just keep away from me," she said. But she said it mechanically, like the words were meaningless.

I shouldn't have stared at her, but I couldn't help myself. Seeing her was reliving again that fleeting moment of sweetness. And that strange, enigmatic expression in her eyes still baffled me. It was as though she wanted to ask a question and doubted I knew the answer.

I was relieved when she looked away from me. She half-turned her shoulder to me, but not so I missed anything when she examined her breast. She knew I could see, because she shot me a quick, up-and-under glance from her blue eyes. But she made no attempt to cover up, took her time tying the broken shoulder-strap. When she got the bodice adjusted, she leaned back on the pillows, lay there curled up, watching me with that same strange expression in her eyes, as though something had happened to her that she didn't understand.

I went through to another bathroom, cleaned up the scratches on my neck and dabbed antiseptic on my cheek where she had bitten it. My neck bothered me most. It was inflamed and painful, skin rubbed raw by the chain. There was nothing I could do except hope it wouldn't get more painful. My arm was still painful. I stripped off my jacket, examined the tiny puncture where the needle had entered. The skin around it was badly inflamed. I touched it tenderly, and darts of pain stabbed through my arm.

An unpleasant suspicion came into my mind. I probed with my fingers, clenched my teeth against the sudden pain twinges.

I went back to my room. The dame was lying on the bed, watching me through half-narrowed eyes.

"I'm going out," I said. "I'm warning you. Just one tricky move, and you're in trouble. I don't wanna be bothered with you. If you're smart and sit quiet, you can have what you want. Try anything smart and you're gonna be chained down so you can't move. Take your choice."

She didn't say anything, just stared.

"D'you want anything?" I asked. "Anything within reason."

"Yes," she said softly. "Get me a newspaper." She was still staring at me.

"Newspapers," I told her tersely, "are what I am going out for."

CHAPTER NINE

I got my car out from the garage, pointed its nose in the direction of town, and arrived some thirty minutes later. It was early afternoon and the mid-day newspapers were on sale. I stopped when I reached the outskirts of town, bought half-a-dozen papers, drank coffee in a drugstore and glanced through the papers slowly and carefully.

Manton's body had been discovered. It was on the second page. Manton's body discovered in a car on the high-road, with two bullet wounds in the chest. Foul play was suspected.

One thing was certain. That news item would get Frisk worried. He'd be even more anxious to find me than the police. The police didn't even know about me! Frisk wouldn't be happy knowing I could put the finger on him at any time.

Two sharp pangs of pain stabbed my arm when I got out dough to pay the check. It was the pain that decided me. I'd have to hide out for a while. I'd buy enough supplies to see me through for a few days while Frisk's men hunted around fruitlessly. And if I was gonna hide out, I'd better do something about this arm.

There was a doctor's surgery nearby. Three folks were already in the surgery. I had to wait half an hour for my turn.

He was a short, podgy guy with hard, earnest eyes. He looked at me like he was trying to see into my brain, and said in firm, precise tones: "You're a stranger around here?"

"That's right," I agreed. "Just passing through. I guess you ..."

"What's the trouble?" He acted like he had a pressing appointment he wanted to keep.

I shrugged off my jacket. "I've got something in my arm," I told him.

He hemmed with a thoughtful air when he saw the discolouration of the skin. He came right up close, tut-tutted some more, levered my arm around. It hurt, and I winced.

"Got something there right enough," he grunted. He prodded some more. "That hurt?"

"Yeah. Sure does."

He stared at me strangely, fumbled in his pocket, pulled out a packet of cigarettes. With an unprofessional rudeness, he lighted a cigarette, walked around his side of the desk and sat down, leaving me standing there with my shirt cuff rolled up.

I watched him through narrowed eyes. He acted like I wasn't there, fumbled in his desk drawer, came up with a diary, which he opened and inspected.

I cleared my throat. "Er ... doctor!"

He looked up. "Well?" His voice was cold.

"If there's something in my arm, maybe I ought to have it out."

"You've got something there, right enough," he said firmly. "What is it?"

I moistened my lips. "Maybe it's a splinter."

He looked at me for a long while, very steadily. "What's your name?"

I licked my lips again. "Richardson," I said. "John Richardson."

"My advice, Mr John Richardson, is go to hospital."

I didn't wanna go to hospital. I wanted my arm doctored so I could get back quick to the house. "There can't be much to it, doctor. Can't you fix it for me?"

He leaned back in his chair, rested his fingers on the desk top. "I'll be frank, Mr Richardson," he said. "You're a drug addict. No, no, no ..." He held up one hand to silence my protest. "You don't have to deny it. I'm a doctor, and I can tell. I can see by your eyes you've recently taken a large dose. But it's not my job to do the work of the police. If you've snapped a needle in your arm, you can go to hospital to have it extracted."

I leaned forward across the desk. "Look, doctor," I pleaded. "Get it out for me, will you? I'll pay you. I'll pay good."

His eyes were suddenly much harder than I'd noticed they could be. "I'm doing you a favour," he said. "You don't know it now. Maybe you'll know sometime. If I take out that piece of needle, you'll go away happily, give yourself other doses.

After a time, you'll become an addict, no hope for you at all."

"So what happens at the hospital?"

"They'll take it out for you," he said quietly. "They'll have a coupla cops around, too. They'll be wanting to know where you got the stuff. You'll have a few questions to answer." He shrugged his shoulders. "I should feel sorry for you, Mr Richardson – but I don't. I've seen enough drug addicts to want the whole system stamped out, those who supply it and those who buy it."

He wasn't arguing. He was just telling me. I reached for my jacket. My arm was hurting a whole lot more now. It was swollen and an angry red.

"I suppose it's no good telling you it was an accident, that I'm not a drug addict?" I asked bitterly.

"Not the slightest," he said smoothly. "My advice is go to hospital. They'll take it out for you."

I glared at him, walked towards the door. I had my hand on the door knob when he called: "Just one more thing, Mr Richardson."

I turned; his eyes were level, his voice firm. "You'll have to go to the hospital, you know. That arm's in a bad way. Signs of blood poisoning."

I glared at him, shut the door behind me and hurried into the street. His words kept re-echoing around in my mind. *Blood poisoning. Blood poisoning. Blood poisoning.* Why, guys could die of blood poisoning. Guys had arms amputated because of blood poisoning!

"*Go to hospital*," he had said. But that was crazy. They'd dig out that needle, but the cops would ask questions. They'd want to know who supplied the dope. Where I came from, where I lived. They might tie me in with Manton's death. They might search my house, find the dame chained up there.

Even if they didn't, they might keep me in jail for weeks. And all the time, the dame would be chained up, slowly dying of thirst and starvation.

I'd have to take a chance. I'd have to wait and see if my arm got better. Maybe the doctor was trying to scare me. Maybe that broken needle would work its own way out.

I pulled my hat down over my eyes, bought up a good stock of provisions and carried them back to the car. As I was thumbing the starter, a newsboy came running along the street yelling out: "Extra. Extra!"

My belly lurched. Maybe it was something new on Manton. I called him over, bought a paper from him. There was a big flaming headline which I barely glanced at. Something about the missing daughter of a millionaire. I skipped the front page, searched for further news of Manton. It was the same report, word for word, as the other papers had it. My belly settled itself. I refolded the paper, tossed it to one side. It fell so I could see a photograph on the front page. It caught my eye. I picked up the paper, stared at the photograph. Then my belly really did lurch. The photograph was of the dame chained up in my room. My fingers were trembling when I opened up the paper, read the headlines once more.

I was in a kinda dream by the time I got through reading it all. Her name was Helen Gaskin. She'd been missing since that morning. While motoring from Chicago to Cleveland, she had simply disappeared, car as well. The police were patrolling all main roads into town and making widespread enquiries.

She was something extra special, was Helen Gaskin. She was extra special on account of her father. He was one of Cleveland's industrialists. They described him as a millionaire. Maybe he didn't have that much dough, but he probably had plenty.

It was the final paragraph that really shook me. The paper stated the police feared Helen Gaskin may have been kidnapped.

Kidnapped!

There was a nasty ring to that word – kidnapped. It had the ring of the clanging of the iron door of the condemned cell. Kidnapping's a capital offence. It used to be a paying proposition to snatch a rich guy's kid and hold it to ransom. A parent would bend over backwards trying not to let the law know he was paying ransom. Once in a while, the kidnappers got the dough and bumped off the kid as well, so they wouldn't run risks of being caught.

Kidnapping became a profitable business, the ransom market became flooded with operators. That's when the government stepped in. They put down kidnapping good and hard. They put it down by the simple expedient of awarding a snatcher the death sentence.

Kidnapped!

I could protest I didn't intend holding Helen to ransom. But she sure was kidnapped. And that's where the rub came. Because if she'd been a thirty-dollar-a-week city typist, it would have been a charge of "*detained against her will*". But Helen's father owned a million bucks. That made my crime a major offence. I was a kidnapper!

It felt like there was wet sand in my belly. Soggy, heavy deposits of sand. I could see what a jam I was in. There was a grave risk that enterprising cops would tie me in with Manton's death. The dame would certainly tie me in with it. And all the time I was imprisoning the dame, I was continuing the offence of kidnapping. And kidnapping was a capital offence!

The world was grey and bleak, with no beginning and no future. Way down the street, I saw a harness cop strolling towards me. It was probably my imagination, but it looked like he was watching me keenly. That dull weight of despair was still heavy in my belly and my head ached. I wondered what I should do, if I should struggle on and hope, or if I should throw in my hand.

The cop was nearer now. He seemed to be watching. Automatically I fumbled for the ignition key, switched on the engine. I slipped in the gear, pulled away from the kerb before the cop reached me. He never so much as I raised his eyes as I passed. I changed gear, headed towards my house. Halfway there, my arm began to throb, and I knew things were really bad.

* * *

She was stretched out on the bed like she'd been asleep when I got upstairs. Seeing her made me forget the throbbing of my arm. She had tiny feet, and they were bare. Her legs were bare, too. Surprisingly bare. I hadn't noticed it quite so forcibly before. She didn't move, lay there watching me through half-closed eyes. It was as though she realized I was watching her, wanted to see my reactions. I put down the box of provisions, pulled the papers from my pocket, selected the one with her photograph on the front page. "That should interest you," I said grimly.

She sat up quickly, grabbed the paper excitedly and pored over it. The cleavage between her breasts was a deep hollow of fascination. I experienced a sudden overwhelming desire to see her close-up the way she had been earlier. Without intending it, I trespassed over the invisible boundary line.

"It's a lousy photograph," she complained. "There's a more recent one than that."

"No photograph would ever do you justice," I said.

Something in my voice got home to her. She slowly turned her head, looked up at me. The same question was still in her eyes, mingled with a kinda unhappiness. "Why did you have to do this?" she asked quietly.

"You saw the way it was," I said. "I didn't kill that guy. They were gonna hang it on me. They doped me, parked me there with the body. That's why I had to stop you squawking."

I could tell by her eyes she didn't believe me. "If you'd wanted money," she said quietly, "you could have got it other ways. You could even have asked me for it."

I moved right up close to her. "You figure I'd planned on kidnapping you?" I asked bluntly.

"Well, didn't you?"

"I didn't know who you were until I saw that photograph." I pointed to the newspaper.

Her eyes were level. "I wish I could believe that."

She was close to me again, white-skinned and perfectly proportioned, the smell of her in my nostrils and the memory of her touch flooding my mind with hot desire. I kept staring until the tension between us became painful. Just a broken shoulder-strap and my memories could be realised.

All at once, I realized she expected to be kissed. It was unbelievable she'd want that, after the way I'd treated her. Understanding and action were fused into one. Her lips were moist and burning, her teeth even and hard. Her arms encircled my neck so fiercely, I knew I was bruising her lips. She was maddeningly exciting, and I wanted to engulf her completely, consume all her sweetness in one wondrous moment. Her body was soft and pliant. I could feel ripples of ecstasy quivering along her back. I nipped the lobe of her ear with my teeth, and she hugged me more urgently. My lips travelled a gentle caressing path down her neck to her white shoulders. There was that hot haze consuming me again, and I was recapturing that same moment of complete happiness.

She broke away abruptly, panting hard, tried to push me away. I didn't want to break. I held her more tightly, locked her fingers in my hair, tugged hard, drawing my head back. She slapped my cheek with her other hand. So hard it startled me, and I let her go. She slapped again then, both hands, each time so hard it was a jolt.

I staggered back a coupla paces, raised my fingers to my stinging cheeks. "What the hell!" I demanded.

She was pulling her shoulder-strap back over her shoulder, cupping her breast with her other hand. Two high spots were burning high up on her cheeks. She was breathing so quickly she could hardly speak. "Keep away from me," she panted.

"Sure," I flared. "I'll keep away from you."

I turned away from her, took a cigarette from my pocket and paced the room a coupla times, furious with her and with myself.

"Don't act that way," she pleaded.

The change in her tone made me stop. There was no animosity in her voice.

I glared at her. "Okay," I said. "I'm sorry about it. It won't happen again."

"Don't act like that," she pleaded.

It was strange how expressive were her eyes. Now they showed pleading, and yes ... just a trace of tenderness.

"I thought you wanted to kiss me," I said gruffly.

"I did," she said simply. She was sitting up on the bed, facing me. Her brief undergarment caught up and strained tautly around her loins, her hands supporting her breasts as though to ease the strain of her laboured breathing.

"What's biting you?" I demanded bluntly.

"It's what I wanted," she said quietly. "But when you kissed me–" Her eyes dropped momentarily and then immediately lifted again, looking at me squarely. "Kissing me like that can lead anywhere."

Just talking about it got the hot haze thick in my head. "You don't have to be my age to know that," I said thickly.

"But it isn't right," she said quickly.

"No?" I said drily.

"Don't you see?" she said pleadingly. She gestured around her. "It isn't right. Not here. Not the way things are." Her fingers played at the chain around her waist. "None of this makes it right. It's got to be just you and me without these other things."

Understanding washed over me then, changing my blood to cold water. This dame was pulling the wool over my eyes. Using her sex, the one weapon I couldn't take away from her. Giving me a high altitude temperature and then a pep talk, all leading up to letting her off that chain.

"You're wasting your time," I growled.

Her eyes were pained. "But it's like that with you, too, isn't it?" she pleaded. "Between us there is ... something!"

"Yeah," I said grimly. "Between us there's a length of chain. And that's staying around your waist. There ain't nothing gonna get you off that chain until I'm good and ready."

She flushed then. A deep flush that stained her cheeks and neck down to her shoulders. Her face became set and hard, and her eyes flamed. "You're just trying to make me feel cheap," she accused.

"Just how cheap can a dame be whose father's a millionaire?" I taunted.

If she'd been standing and wearing high-heeled shoes, she'd have stamped her foot with impotent fury. As it was, she rolled over on her side, pounded her fist angrily on the pillow. The chain clanked in musical unison.

"I've got eggs," I grunted. "D'you like omelette?"

She sat up, glared at me resentfully. "Do I have to beg for it?"

"All part of the service."

Now I'd cooled down, I was beginning to notice the throbbing of my arm. I stripped off my jacket, inspected it. It was much more swollen, the skin much redder, maybe with a yellowy tinge! But maybe that was my imagination. Not only was it throbbing perpetually, it was stabbing fire every time I moved my arm. I didn't replace my jacket, I prepared a meal using my good arm, resting the other one. She saw me inspecting my bad arm, but didn't say anything. Maybe she thought it was an injury caused by her that same morning.

I fed her, fed her good. When she was through, I cleared the things away, relaxed in a chair and held a match for her so she could light a cigarette.

She curled up on the bed in her customary position, blew smoke through her nostrils and stared at me through half-closed eyes. "Who are you, anyway?" she asked.

I shrugged my shoulders. "Does it matter? Lee Shelton is the name I'm known by."

"Lee," she said thoughtfully. She said it again. "Lee." Listened to the sound of it, as though judging its quality. "It's a nice name," she decided.

"Yeah," I said. "It's a nice name." I moved, and winced as my arm stabbed with pain.

"Just how long d'you reckon to keep me here?" she demanded.

I thought it over. "Depends," I said. "Like I told you, I was framed for murdering somebody. I can duck out for that. But there's a guy I've gotta settle with first."

"What do you mean? Duck out?"

I grinned easily. "You're the only one who can tie me in with that dead man. I can take my car, cross the border and send a telegram to the cops telling them where to find you."

Her eyes were thoughtful. She was giving it consideration. She said, slowly: "If these men did frame you, why don't you duck out now?" She leaned forward eagerly. "If you want to do that, I promise not to tell the cops anything about you. Nothing at all."

I looked at her steadily, grinned evilly. "I could duck out without telling about you. You'd stay here until you got so thin you could slip out of that chain."

"You wouldn't do that," she said quickly. She sounded worried.

"No," I said. "I wouldn't do that."

"What are you waiting for?" she urged. "Why don't you get going? As soon as you're across the State line, you could telegraph father, tell him where to find me. And I mean it. I wouldn't tell anybody anything about you." Her eyes were earnest, appealing. "I really do mean it. You do believe me?"

"I'm not ready to duck out," I said grimly. "I've got things to settle first."

Her eyes narrowed: "What things?"

Maybe the smouldering hate and anger was gleaming in my eyes. The anger was always with me; living with me, sleeping with me, growing inside me all the time. "There's a guy I've gotta settle with," I said grimly.

"The man who tried to frame you?"

"That's him," I said bitterly. "I've gotta settle with him."

"It's eating away inside you, isn't it, Lee?" she said swiftly. "It's festering there. Something he did. Something that hurt you pretty bad."

I gritted my teeth. "Sure," I said. "I hate him pretty much." I wasn't hearing or seeing her. I was seeing Frisk's face, and my hand clenched like I was gonna take a sock at him.

"What did he do to you, Lee?" she asked quietly. "What can a man do to make you feel so bad about him?"

"It wouldn't interest you."

"But I am interested." She clambered around on that bed like a kitten. She'd turned around now, resting her feet on the pillow and her elbows supporting her chin at the foot of the bed. "Tell me what he did, Lee," she encouraged.

"You wouldn't believe it, anyway," I growled.

"Tell me just the same."

It was the expression in her eyes that got me talking. Somehow in the last half-hour she'd changed, become a different person, warm and friendly, almost a good pal.

"It happened a long while ago," I said.

CHAPTER TEN

I'd disliked Frisk on sight. Even though I was just a kid, ten years of age, I'd instinctively distrusted him.

It was different for my mother. She'd been a widow for eight years. I guess she'd got tired of living alone, and Frisk could be charming with women when he put himself out. He put himself out as far as my mother was concerned. I was horror-stricken when my mother first told me I was going to have a new father, and that I must learn to obey and respect him.

Being just a kid of ten, I didn't realize the significance of everything. But in later years, thinking back, I was able to tie up the odd little things that happened, realize and fully understand exactly how Frisk tortured and drove my mother to death.

In the first place, he lied to her about his financial position. He was always smartly, flashily dressed, and during his brief courtship was constantly buying orchids and candies for my mother. But from the day he brought her back from the church as his bride, everything changed with breathtaking suddenness.

Previously, he had been charming, suave and ingratiating. Now he was domineering, smilingly cruel and utterly selfish. I remember distinctly the wedding day. There was no honeymoon, on account I had to go to school and mother would not leave me to fend for myself. There was no wedding party, because none of my mother's relatives would acknowledge Frisk. Frisk himself had no personal friends he wanted to invite.

The three of us sat at table, and the coloured maid served tea. Mother said, looking at him tenderly: "When will our furniture be arriving, John, dear?"

He smiled that smile I grew to know so well and hate. "It's outside in the hall."

My mother stared at him. "Just two suitcases?"

"That's right."

"But the other stuff you have. The furniture you're so proud of. When will that be coming? We must make room for it."

Again that smile. "There is no furniture, my dear."

My mother stared at him, forehead crinkling in perplexity.

"Perhaps now is the best time to tell you," he said calmly. "I am a pauper. I have come to the end of my resources." His kindly eyes smiled at my mother. "Our union for that reason alone is highly gratifying to me."

My mother had money. She owned the house we lived in and had securities and annuities that would take care of her for the rest of her life.

"You're joking, John," she said. She gave a timid little laugh. "You're pulling my leg."

"I was never more serious, my dear. I'm entirely reliant upon you. I have no income, no job."

Again my mother's perplexed frown. "But why, John? You've always had plenty of money, you told me your job was ..."

"My money, my dear!" he interrupted. "You think only of money. Now I've told you ..."

"But that's not fair," she burst out. "It's just such a surprise you didn't tell me this earlier."

He shrugged his shoulders. "Well, you know now." Again that smile. "Doubtless we shall work out something between us."

That was the beginning. Right from the first, he made it clear to mother he'd married her for her money, although right then she probably didn't realize what he was telling her. Later that evening, he made it abundantly clear what he thought of her in other ways.

For an hour or more, mother and I had been playing cards. Frisk, who declined to play, sat smoking a cigar, drumming his fingers on the table impatiently. Finally he pulled out his watch, consulted it and ordered: "All right, Lee. Up to bed now."

I looked at him indignantly. "It's too early for me to go to bed."

He looked at me steadily. "Don't argue, boy. Up to bed when I tell you."

Mother intervened. “But John, dear. It’s early yet. He never goes up until later than this.”

He stared at her levelly. “You’re going to bed, too,” he said meaningfully.

She laughed like he was joking. “But John, dear, I don’t want to go to bed yet.”

“I do,” he said heavily.

She flashed a quick glance at me and looked back to Frisk warningly. “Lee will go to bed presently. We’ll follow him.”

She musta been embarrassed. My father died when I was two. It was gonna be a new experience for her to take a man up to her bedroom.

Frisk’s voice didn’t change its inflection. It was still mild and gentle. “My dear. We’re going to bed now. For three months you’ve been boasting about your spotless moral behaviour. I cannot wait to enjoy the advantages of your stored-up, hidden passions.” His voice was mocking and cynical. Mother’s cheeks stained red. She said, sharply: “John. Please. The boy!”

Right then, I didn’t understand the words he used. But I sensed they were hurtful to my mother. I glowered at him.

“You have been so arrogant, so proud of your purity,” he mocked. “It is my intention now to humble that pride, shatter your illusions that I respect shy and retiring womanhood.”

Mother was on her feet, her cheeks flaming. “Stop, John,” she burst out. Her hand thumped the table. “Don’t dare talk that way.”

He was easy and unconcerned. He turned his head casually, stared at me. “Go to bed.”

I sat there, glowered at him.

“Very well, my dear,” he said mildly. “I will describe in detail exactly what will take place from the moment we arrive in our bedroom. In the first place, I shall ...”

Mother turned white. She swayed, placed her hand to her forehead. She said, quietly: “Lee; kiss mother goodnight and go to bed.”

“I don’t want to go to bed,” I protested.

“Be a good boy, Lee,” she insisted. “Kiss mother goodnight and go to bed now.”

I went to bed reluctantly. And, of course, I didn't stay there. Wearing pyjamas, I crept out of my bedroom, spied on them. I was curious, like all kids.

And what I saw sowed the first germs of hatred of Frisk inside me. It was happening in our dining-room, my mother, with flushed face and shamed eyes, pleading with him while he made her submit to embraces that were loathsome and horrible.

To me, it was the end of the world. My mother, my gentle, kindly, lady-like mother, with that man under such circumstances! For weeks, I couldn't bear the shame of it, slunk away from the other boys at school, hid myself whenever possible, always afraid someone would see in my eyes that I knew of these horrible things.

From the day they were married, it was a divided home, Frisk coming between my mother and me like a grim shadow, and always lounging around the house, smoking or inviting his newly-found friends to play cards. Often there were wild parties and I was locked in my bedroom. In the morning, the dining-room would smell of cigar smoke and be littered with empty bottles.

In later years, I linked together the bits and pieces of information, the scraps of conversation I overheard and remembered. Much too late, I understood the deadly, merciless nature of Frisk's plans.

It was mother's dough Frisk was after. But when she realized his true character, she fought him, kept control of her property and income.

The fact she refused to pass control of her estate to Frisk was a constant bone of contention. She managed her own affairs, gave Frisk a small allowance with which to gamble and drink but paid all the housekeeping bills and the cost of his wild parties. She'd resigned herself to having a husband without morals or scruples. And she suffered. She must have suffered terribly in his lewd embrace, knowing from his own lips that he had come direct from another woman's arms. A woman who had been bought with her money!

Maybe it would have been different if mother had given Frisk half or even three-quarters of what she owned, on condition he left her. But she didn't. She held on grimly to her property, telling herself her husband had left it for her.

It was when Frisk had been in our house six months that the doctor arrived. He was a tall, thin, hawk-nosed man with a bald head and a pronounced stoop. He had one very blue eye that was out of focus and constantly watering. The other eye was greyish-green.

Frisk called him "Doc Morgan." Despite mother's protests, he moved in, occupied one of the spare bedrooms, which he littered with cheroot stubs. He flung them on the floor casually, not always bothering to extinguish them. Other changes took place. The coloured maid was dismissed and replaced by a younger girl, who lived on the premises. I understood only in later years why that coloured girl was always laughing and mocking mother, and why mother avoided speaking to her if possible, walked past her with eyes averted.

It was shortly after Doc Morgan arrived that mother began to be ill. She didn't look ill, but Frisk told her she was ill. So did Doc Morgan. They said she should take things easy, not worry too much. I was just a kid, but I remembered funny things that happened. One day, mother would be looking for her purse. She couldn't find it anywhere. The next day, I'd find it in the chicken-coop, or maybe the coloured maid would find it in the gas-oven.

These kinda things happened frequently. And all the time, Doc Morgan and Frisk were telling mother she shouldn't worry, said she should rest, lie down and not upset herself. I remember the time mother was in the lounge, asking Frisk if he had seen her glasses. He looked at her, puzzled. "But you just took them outside with you, my dear."

"I haven't worn them all day," she told him.

Frisk looked at Doc Morgan. Morgan shrugged his stooped shoulders. "You shouldn't get so excited, Mrs Frisk," he said gently.

She stared at him. She sounded desperate. "What are you trying to tell me?" she asked.

Frisk said bluntly: "You've been wearing your glasses all morning. Just ten minutes ago, you took them off, put them in the spectacle case and went out to the kitchen with them."

She stared at him, pressed her hand to her head. "But I haven't …" she began faintly.

Doc Morgan leaned forward slightly. His one good eye was fastened on her, intently. "What was that, Mrs Frisk?"

She looked at him with wild, desperate eyes. "I just don't know what I could have done with them," she gasped. She hurried out of the room, nervously fumbling for her handkerchief in her apron pocket. That kinda thing was happening day after day, Mother not remembering, hiding things away where she couldn't find them.

It was three months later when Dr Manders arrived from Chicago. I knew there was something special going on, because I was kept out of the way. Frisk and the two doctors talked alone together for a long time. While they were talking, my mother was very upset, crying all the time. Afterwards, Frisk came out, and she went to see the two doctors by herself. Frisk caught sight of me, beckoned me over, wagged his finger at me solemnly. "Listen, boy," he said. "You've got to understand, your mother's ill. You mustn't worry her. D'you understand?"

I scowled at him. "You made her ill," I said. I had no logical reason for saying it. I just felt it, deep down in my childish mind. For a moment his face hardened, then his kindly smile shone out. He fumbled in his pocket. "Here's a dollar," he said. "Go buy yourself some sweets."

I was just a kid. A dollar was all the dough in the world. I forgot everything in my hurry to get to the candy store.

When I got back, mother was upstairs in her bedroom. I was told she wasn't to be disturbed, must have complete rest. All her meals were taken to her room by the coloured maid, by Frisk or by one of the two doctors. The bedroom door was always locked.

The next day, the workmen arrived. It was all excitement to me. I didn't understand, didn't try to understand why the small, bare room at the top of the house should be fitted with bars, chains stapled to the walls and the door reinforced and fitted with a grille. I never saw mother for another fortnight. Many times I rattled her bedroom door but got no reply. Once, after she'd been served with a meal, I was able to creep up the stairs, look through the keyhole. I could see mother lying in bed. She looked terribly white and pale. Dr Morgan was bending over her. He had a hypodermic and was injecting her arm.

But a fortnight later, Doc Morgan and Doc Manders solemnly took me into the dining-room. They closed the door carefully, regarded me very seriously. Morgan fixed me with his one good eye, looked down his nose and said: "Young man, you've got to be brave."

I swallowed. "What's happened to Mum?" I pleaded. "What are you doing to her?"

Manders turned away, coughed. Morgan's one good eye stared at me levelly. "D'you know what insane means, my boy?" he asked abruptly.

"Insane!"

The word frightened me. It conjured up pictures of raving lunatics snapping iron shackles, rending flesh with bare teeth and striking out with maniacal strength. I nodded dumbly, the shadow of apprehension creeping over me.

He shook his head sadly. "You must be brave, my boy," he said. "Your mother is ... insane!"

I didn't believe it. Wouldn't believe it. I sobbed hysterically, punched at him, fought to get out of the room and to get up to mother's bedroom. But they held me, tried to reason with me, and finally locked me in my bedroom to cry into the long, long night.

That was when it became a hideous reality. My mother, insane! That was the reason for the room at the top of the house to which she was transferred. I was never allowed to see her. A door was built halfway up the final flight to the attic. Only the doctors and Frisk had the key of that door and could go beyond it. The weeks passed, and I was tortured by the desire to see Mother, and afraid of what I would see when I did see her.

Many times I hovered on the stairs, watched as Frisk or one of the doctors opened that door, carefully locking it behind them before disappearing into the upper regions of the house. Time and again, I pleaded to be allowed to see Mother. Always it was the same answer. It was better for me not to see her.

The weeks passed into months. Almost eighteen months had elapsed since Frisk had married mother. Eighteen months of hell and misery.

Then I got my opportunity. It was a Saturday afternoon. The key of that door was kept by Frisk in his vest pocket. He and the two doctors had been playing cards, smoking heavily and drinking too much. Finally the game broke up, Dr Morgan went up to his room and Frisk and Manders fell asleep in their chairs.

I had the courage of desperation. I crept into the room on my hands and knees, crept alongside Frisk's chair, and with trembling fingers fumbled in his waistcoat pocket, my heart leaping wildly as I found the key.

I hardly dared to breathe as I crept up the stairs, fitted the key in the lock and felt it open. Then there was nothing to stop me. Yet, having got so far, I was afraid. I crept up the stairs, stood staring for long minutes at the sturdy wooden door behind which I knew she was imprisoned.

I found the courage to open the door. At first, it seemed like the room was empty. It was filthy, smelled abominably. In the far corner, beneath the window, a bundle of rags moved and stirred. There was something horrible about the way it moved. I would have turned and run had fear not taken the strength from my legs. The bundle moved again, so that now I could see it was a living person. It scrambled to its feet and, as I stared horror-stricken, a weak voice croaked, "Lee. My boy!"

There was a chain around her waist that allowed her practically no movement. The single garment she wore, like her hair, was so matted with the filth of her own excrement, in which she was forced to lie, that it was indistinguishable from any other part of her body. She knelt there, arms outstretched towards me, and only her burning eyes were recognisable.

"Lee," she sobbed. "My boy," she cried. "Come to me."

Often have I regretted what I did then. But I was just a kid. She was my mother, and I knew it. But she was repulsive and horrible. The yearning inside me was opressed by her revolting aspect.

"What are they doing to you, Mum?" I asked timidly.

"Come to me, Lee," she pleaded.

I took only a coupla paces towards her. The smell was worse the nearer I got. "What are they doing to you?" I asked again.

She musta seen the expression on my face and understood. She asked, quickly: "How did you get up here?"

"I stole the key," I said. "They wouldn't let me come."

"They don't know you're here, then?"

I shook my head.

"Be a good boy, Lee," she said, panting with excitement. "Go to the police-station. You know where it is. Tell them what you've seen. Tell them I'm imprisoned. Say they're trying to drive me crazy. Will you do that, Lee? Will you go at once?"

I stared at her in amazement. "You mean it isn't true? You're not really ill?"

"Believe me, Lee," she said, her voice breaking. "It's a trick. They're trying to drive me mad. John wants to get control of my property. He can do that if they drive me mad." Her voice was suddenly angry. "That's what they're doing, Lee. They're trying to drive me mad. I can't hold on much longer."

I was just a kid. "You mean, go to the police-station?" I said, appalled.

"That's right, Lee," she urged. Her eyes were suddenly shining with hope. "Go right away. Tell them exactly what you've seen. And hurry. Hurry."

I hurried. I crept down the stairs, fastened the door behind me, dropped the yale key on the floor outside the lounge, where Frisk would be sure to find it and think he had dropped it accidentally. Then I set off for the police-station, running as fast as I knew how. Mother had told me to hurry.

I can't say I blamed the cops. What was I? A kid, not yet twelve years of age. I ran breathless into the police-station, stammered out some wild, incredible story of my mother being chained up in a locked room.

At first they tried to send me away. Then, when I became insistent, they got annoyed. When they saw I wasn't afraid of their threats to lock me in a cell if I didn't stop telling lies, the desk sergeant shrugged his shoulders wearily. "Okay, Flartery," he said. "Take the kid home. Find out what it's about."

Now I had the hefty, protecting bulk of Flartery beside me, I couldn't get home fast enough. I kept hurrying ahead, urging him to hurry. He acted like he didn't hear me, walked slowly and ponderously, his keen eyes watching the traffic, the hawkers, the loitering bookmaker's runners and everybody except me.

Finally we did get home. He looked at the long drive leading up towards the house. "This where you live, kid?" he asked, doubtfully. I could tell he thought I was lying.

"This is the place," I said urgently. "Hurry."

He reached out, rested his hand on my shoulder. He didn't do it in a friendly way, rather as though to make sure I didn't run away. We walked up the drive together, his slow, ponderous tread grinding the gravel loudly.

It was Frisk who opened the door. I was watching him triumphantly. I saw the momentary flash of surprise in his face when he saw the cop had his hand on my shoulder. Then he was smooth, slick and courteous. "Good evening, officer. Is there ... trouble?" He broke off, looked at me meaningfully.

The cop's fingers tightened on my shoulder. "D'you know this boy?"

Frisk took so long looking at me, I thought he was going to deny he knew me. Finally he said wearily: "What is it this time, officer?"

The way he said "*this time*" implied I was always in trouble. The cop breathed heavily. "You're his father?"

"Step-father," corrected Frisk politely.

The cop said: "Could I see his mother. Have a talk with her?"

Frisk said: "Good lord!" abruptly, and raised his eyes to heaven. Then he heaved a deep sigh. "Don't tell me he's come to you with *that* story."

The cop stared at him. "You know about it?"

Frisk tut-tutted and shook his head despairingly. "I can't make up my mind whether he's stupid or deliberately malicious."

The cop said, obstinately: "I'd like to see his mother. He says she's chained up." Then his face and tone softened. "Not that we believe him, of course. But it's our duty to check these things."

"Naturally," said Frisk easily. He widened the door, called aloud: "Dr Morgan. Can you come here a moment?"

Dr Morgan musta been behind the door listening. He appeared promptly. "Trouble, Mr Frisk?" he asked.

Frisk's voice implied he was unutterably weary of me. "The boy again," he said. "The same story."

Dr Morgan gave me a long, thoughtful stare. "I warned you, Mr Frisk," he said. "The boy needs special treatment."

I wrenched myself away from the cop, pushed past Frisk and Morgan. Having succeeded so far, I was desperate to prove myself. I yelled to the cop: "It's this way. Up these stairs. Come and see for yourself."

The cop remained standing on the doorstep like his feet were rooted there. I was almost crying with frustration. "You've gotta come," I pleaded. "This way. Come with me. You can see for yourself." I was halfway to the staircase now.

Frisk's voice cut through my words with sudden loud and dominating fury. "Come back here, boy. Don't you dare disobey your instructions. I won't have you worrying your mother."

Dr Manders appeared suddenly, manoeuvred around behind me, caught me by the shoulders and held me tight. His voice was gentle, although his grip on my shoulders was steely. "You must be a good boy," he reasoned. "You don't want to make your mother worse."

Morgan said quickly: "Perhaps I had better make the position clear, officer. My name is Morgan." He paused for effect. "Dr Morgan." He gestured towards me. "This is my colleague, Dr Manders. We've been called in by Mr Frisk. We shall be staying here as long as her condition is critical."

The cop asked: "You mean his mother's ill?"

Doc Morgan nodded. "The boy's at an impressionable age. We can't expect him to understand these things. His mother's in a bad nervous state, requires absolute rest. We're in constant attention upon her. The boy's mischievous and troublesome. He's a great worry to her, and for her own sake we keep him away from her." He sighed, shrugged his shoulders. "I regret it's no good explaining to him our reasons. He's very obstinate."

The cop looked embarrassed. You could almost hear his mind ticking as he figured things out. Finally he asked: "You're Doc Morgan?"

"That's right."

The cop looked towards me. "And you're Dr Manders?"

Manders nodded over me. "Dr Morgan called me in on this case," he said smoothly. "A most interesting case. A rare type of nervous phenomenon. The patient requires absolute rest and constant medical attention. That way, she may pull through."

The cop swallowed. "I'm sorry, gentlemen," he said. "But you see, we have to do our duty, and when that kid ..."

Manders said, smoothly: "Of course, officer. We quite understand." He looked across at Morgan. "I don't think it will be wise," he doubted. "But if the officer would like to see Mrs Frisk ..."

Morgan looked doubtful. "I wouldn't advise it. But if the officer feels his duty ..."

The cop said quickly: "I can take you gentlemen's word for it." His forefinger eased his collar. He got suddenly angry. "It's that damned kid," he said. "Turned the station upside down."

Frisk said, smoothly: "We shall take the necessary steps, officer. I don't think you will be bothered with him any more."

The cop glared at me ferociously. "You orta be ashamed of yourself," he snarled. "Your poor mother lying ill and you causing all this trouble. Just let me see you down the station again, and the sergeant will give you the taste of a cell."

Frisk said quickly: "I would heartily support you, officer. I shall do my best to make sure he does not bother you again. But if it should occur," he paused meaningfully, "two or three hours in a cell might convince him it's painful to continually tell lies and cause trouble."

The cop said, evenly: "He's your son. And if that's what you want, we'll do it like a shot."

Doc Morgan said: "His parents have been too lenient with him. He's had too much of his own way. I think your suggestion would be admirable."

Frisk said: "I'm sorry about the trouble you've been caused, officer." He moved closer to him, paper rustled, and the cop's face became smiling and contented. He saluted, said goodnight politely, and as he closed the door behind him, Frisk mopped his forehead.

"Jeepers. That was close!"

Morgan looked at Manders. "You got me sweating blood," he said. "If he'd wanted to see her, we'd have been finished."

Manders said, smoothly: "If he'd insisted, we could have gone up first, found the patient too dangerously ill."

Frisk said, with sudden vehemence: "It's going on too long. It's too dangerous. How's she managing to hold out?"

"She's a strong-willed woman," said Morgan. "But she's gotta crack any time now. Nobody could stand up to that treatment long."

Manders said, warningly: "The kid!"

They all looked at me then. Frisk's, Morgan's and Manders' eyes piercing into my brain. I was suddenly terrified.

"Telling lies, eh?" said Frisk, and his eyes narrowed.

"Have to teach him a lesson," said Morgan.

They both moved towards me. I struggled, tried to squirm away from them. And then they carried me, screaming, fighting and kicking, upstairs to my bedroom. My memory of what happened afterwards is enveloped in a red haze of pain and fever. They were three full-grown men. I was a child. They stripped me, held me down and took turns to whip me with a leather strap; I guess they belted me near to death, because I was delirious, enmeshed in wild, nightmare dreams as my body writhed in eternal fire. There were flashes of consciousness when it was morning or night, and one or other of them was forcing food into my mouth. I guess it would have been too dangerous if I'd died on them.

That beating had its effect. It imprinted indelibly on my mind absolute fear and terror of all three of them. Weeks later, when I was at last allowed out of my bedroom, my body no longer showing the signs of my beating, I limped downstairs, beaten and humiliated, flinching from the slightest movement any of them made, desperately resolved not to say or do anything that would bring such suffering on me again.

Yeah, I was reduced into a mass of whimpering nerves, frightened even of my own shadow. I went to school, was shunned by my school-mates, who no longer wanted my company. After school, obeying Frisk's instructions obediently, I returned home and was locked in my bedroom with books or toys. Never again would I dare to disobey Frisk.

It was three months afterwards when the inevitable happened. Frisk and the doctors were upstairs a great deal now. They were taking up pails of hot, steaming water, soap and towels and disinfectant. The coloured maid was busy too, cooking delicate and appetising food. I didn't understand all this activity then. But I understood it later. Mother had finally broken. Her tortured brain had stood up to the inhuman treatment longer than could reasonably be expected. Now, at last, her mind had revolted, snapped beneath the inhuman strain. Having driven her to insanity, they were now eliminating all trace of their inhuman behaviour, washing and cleaning mother, feeding her with delicate, nourishing foods so she should appear physically healthy and well-nourished.

The end came the weekend Doc Morgan and Dr Manders went away. The truth was, of course, that neither of them were doctors, just friends of Frisk.

I was there when Frisk called in another doctor. I was there when the ambulance arrived and white-coated men entered the bedroom, to which my mother had now been returned. I saw her when they brought her out wearing the strange garment that was called a straitjacket. Her thin lips were rolled back to show sharp teeth, her eyes wild and her hair dishevelled. Worst of all were the flecks of foam at the corner of her mouth.

To watch Frisk, you'd have thought he was the most upset guy in the world. He was a broken man, almost on the verge of weeping. The doctor patted him kindly on the shoulder before he went away with the ambulance.

What did I do? I slunk in a corner as far away from Frisk as I could get, watching him with hunted eyes, flinching at any quick movements of his hands.

Frisk got legal authority to assume control of his wife's property. Shortly afterwards, the house was put up for sale. Frisk bought a nightclub, moved me over there. To me, the routine was no different. I went to school, returned obediently and was locked in my bare bedroom with my homework. Right through the night I'd lie awake, listening to the strains of the jazz-band, shrinking in terror whenever I heard footsteps outside my door.

When I was fourteen and no longer obliged to go to school, Frisk put me in the kitchen, washing-up and polishing knives and forks. I saw Dr Manders only once more. That was when he returned after Mother had been taken to the asylum. He stopped two days, disappeared again. Doc Morgan went away with him, but turned up again some time later. He seemed to dog Frisk, follow him everywhere. And they weren't friends any longer. Frisk hated him. But Morgan hung around like he was amused with life and had some secret hold over Frisk.

Mother died shortly after I was fourteen. Frisk mentioned it to me casually. Told me she'd died two or three days before. I didn't cry. I was too young to understand it all then. But there was nothing to hold me with Frisk any more. The next day, when I got my opportunity, I stole a few dollars from the till. I left town, travelled overland as far as the dollars would take me. I wound up in a small, wayside station. A farmer gave me work helping with the harvest, and from then on, I was on my own.

Working in the open air helped me to grow stronger and healthy. I quit farming, went to town and got myself a job with a construction contractor. Later, I studied at evening school, spent all my time studying. I worked well, and was rewarded. By the time I was twenty-five, I was holding down a promising job. I was getting good money, too. But I lived frugally, saved my money. Because, as the years passed and my memories lived with me, I realized exactly what Frisk had done to Mother. That left just one thought in my mind. Revenge!

During those years, I kept track of Frisk, knew when he moved to Cleveland and started this new nightclub. I paid plenty of dough to guys to get me information about Frisk. I knew the money he was making, the sound financial position he was building himself into, and knew it was all due to the money he had killed Mother in order to obtain.

Finally, when I'd saved enough money, I gave up my job, travelled to Cleveland with just one thought in my mind. I was gonna make Frisk suffer as he'd made Mother suffer. I was gonna imprison him, chain him down until his mind too cracked beneath the strain, until he too was dragged into an asylum, his arms imprisoned in a straitjacket and his jaws foaming like a wild beast.

Revenge was my reason for being in Cleveland. Revenge was my reason for that damp cellar, the heavy chains and the isolation of this house. A house so isolated that a half-mad man could shake his chains and howl into the long night like a wolf without attracting attention.

CHAPTER ELEVEN

It was a wild, incredible story to tell anyone. Only I, who had lived through it, could understand the way it happened. Yet it was a relief to give Helen a rough outline of the revenge I'd planned and my reasons. I'd never told anyone this before. Talking about it now eased the strain of it, helped me to understand that my deliberate, cold-blooded revenge was just retribution.

I couldn't tell if she believed me or not. She wasn't looking at me, was tracing a pattern on the eiderdown with her finger. Without looking up, she asked: "What happened to the two doctors?"

"I traced Manders," I said dully. "He died before Mother died. Doc Morgan was different. He came back to Frisk, hung around. I don't doubt he was after more dough. Frisk probably fixed him."

"What happened to him?"

"Died in a car smash," I said. "Was said to have been drunk at the time. Crashed through a fence, went over an embankment."

"You don't believe it was an accident?" she asked quietly.

"I don't care," I said bitterly. "It's enough to know he's dead."

"Can you prove any of this?" she asked. "Aren't there witnesses, people who will bear out what you say? Can't you take him to court?"

I smiled grimly. "There isn't a thing I could prove. Maybe I could have proved it then, had I been old enough." I got angry. "What the hell do I wanna prove anyway? I want Frisk to suffer as Mother suffered. He won't do that in court."

She looked up, eyed me steadily. "That man I saw in the car," she said. "You say you were framed, that you didn't murder him."

"They killed him," I said wearily. "They doped me, left me in the car with him. They wanted the cops to find me. Pin it on me."

"Was it Frisk who killed him?"

I nodded. "That's the irony of it," I said bitterly. "I came here to get Frisk, take my revenge. He didn't even recognise me. Yet he framed me, put me in as tough a spot as he did Mother."

She said quickly: "Why don't you let me go? I won't say as I saw you. I've got money. I'll try to help you."

I looked at her. I remembered the way she'd never stopped fighting me, the way she'd struggled all the time there was a chance she might get away. I remembered how she'd ripped her dress to pieces, risked her neck climbing through that window. Then finally, with the chain around her waist and the realization that escape was hopeless, she'd tried to strangle me and beat my head in. Later she'd tried to use her undoubtedly beautiful body to obtain her release.

Now she was trying just one more angle, pretending to sympathize with me, hoping I might be sucker enough release her so she could bring the police down around my ears.

I got up, shrugged on my jacket. I had to grit my teeth against the pain of my arm.

"Where are you going?" she demanded.

"Get the evening papers," I told her. "I wanna see if there's anything new."

There wasn't anything new. Only that Manton's daughter, Jessica, had been to the morgue to identify him. She'd come accompanied by a friend and had collapsed, had to be taken home semiconscious.

The rest of the paper was full of the search for Helen Gaskin. There were pictures of her on every page. Helen at Monte Carlo, Helen riding to hounds across rural English countryside, Helen bob-sledging at the winter-sports, Helen in her racing car on the sands in Florida.

There was a reward of twenty-five thousand dollars for information about Helen. The police had no doubt she'd been kidnapped. Helen and her car had disappeared as completely as if they'd been snatched from the highroads by a giant hand. But the police had got several leads, which they were following closely. They were convinced her release and the capture of her kidnappers was imminent.

I knew that was newspaper talk. But it got me worried. I drove back to the house with my collar turned up and with the uneasy feeling that everyone I passed was staring at me with recognition in their eyes.

She was in the bathroom when I got back. "It's all right," she called. "I'm not escaping. I'm washing."

"Feeling hungry?"

"Rather!"

"Corned beef and baked beans."

She was disappointed. "It's better than nothing, I suppose."

I took off my jacket, winced with the pain of my arm, which was severely swollen, and set about preparing a meal. It was almost ready by the time she came out. Her face was clean and shiny, like she'd rubbed it hard with the towel. But her hair was dishevelled and her lips pale. That didn't make her look any the less attractive. She approached me as near as the chain would allow, leaned forward so she could inspect what I was doing.

"Anything I can do?" she asked.

I grunted. "I'm managing." I was wishing she hadn't torn that dress. Having been so close to her, and having her around now in an undergarment so cunningly revealing, meant she was constantly on my mind. Not that I minded it. But I had to be careful, remember she was cool and calculating, remember she was waiting her opportunity, willing to sacrifice trump cards if she could win the game.

Yeah, I was plenty worried. I hadn't bothered much with dames, had never been much in their company. I was scared just how far I might lose control of myself with this one.

"Why not let me do the cooking?" she asked. "Push the stove over here with the provisions. I'll throw together something tasty. I'm really good, you know."

Her blue eyes looked at me, wide and sincere. Then she flushed as I sneered. "D'you think I'm crazy? You'd burn the house down if you got your hands on that stove. You'd cut my throat if I let you have a knife."

Her shoulders kinda drooped. She turned away from me, went back to the bed and sat on it, dangling her legs rather like a naughty little girl who's just been scolded. Immediately I felt sorry, wanted to apologise. But I wouldn't let myself. I wasn't gonna give way to her at any point.

"You said it would be better for us both if I resigned myself to being here," she pouted.

"Are you resigned to it?"

She shrugged her shoulders. "I guess I can't do anything about it."

"First chance you get, you'll make a break," I said.

She flared at me viciously. "D'you blame me? Your mother was chained up the way I am. It drove her crazy. D'you blame me for wanting to get away?"

"You won't be here that long," I promised. "Just as soon as I've settled with Frisk and evened the score, I'll duck out."

"How long's that gonna take?" she asked bitterly. "You've waited fifteen years already. How many more years?"

"Just a few days."

"Just how do you intend to do it?"

I didn't have an answer to that. My one hope had been to get Frisk alone. That hope was doomed now. Frisk had plenty of enemies. Wherever he went, he had Gunn and Jenks for his bodyguards. Kidnapping Frisk and getting him to this house was gonna be a superhuman task.

I pushed a plate of food across the boundary line. "That's the best I can do," I grunted.

"You're such a fool," she complained. "Why don't you let me cook something? I can't possibly get away while there's this." Her fingers toyed with the chain, clinked it irritably.

"Eat that," I said. "That's all you'll get."

She got off the bed, picked up the plate and looked at it. Her lips curled in a sneer. "You don't really mean you're going to keep serving me with this kinda ..."

"Shuddup and eat it," I said.

The indignant way she stared showed she'd never been spoken to that way before. Her eyes widened with indignation and fury. She lost her temper. "Why you conceited ..." Words choked in her throat.

"Shuddup," I said. "Pipe down and eat up."

She had been spoiled as a kid. She acted almost without thinking. I ducked as the plate whistled at my head. It smashed against the wall, hot gravy and beans spattered floor and ceiling. I straightened up, glared at her. She glared back, defiantly. Then suddenly she was ashamed of herself. "I'm sorry," she said, penitently. "I lost my temper."

"You lost your supper, too!"

"I didn't mean to act that way," she apologised. "Please forgive me. It's just that I'm not used to being spoken to the way you spoke to me."

I grunted, sat down and started eating. When I was halfway through, she said: "I did offer to do the cooking myself. Can I cook something else?"

"I gave you supper," I growled. "You've had it."

The throb of my arm was becoming unbearable. That's why I was getting so bad-tempered myself. I finished eating, put away the plates. She sat watching me expectantly. She was hungry. But she had too much pride to ask again for food.

Maybe I would have relented, given her something to eat. But she got up, said something very loud, very unladylike and very rude, and stalked through to the bathroom. She jammed the door closed as far as she could. It was the nearest she could get to walking out on me.

The pain in my arm was becoming impossible. I took a bottle of whisky from the cabinet, found a box of aspirins and went along the passage to one of the other rooms. In front of the mirror, I carefully inspected my arm. It was swollen, the flesh reddened, and a tiny yellow spot showed around the scab caused where the needle point had entered. I took four aspirins, washed them down with whisky. Then I went back to her room, took a blanket from her bed, settled in an armchair and drank another large slug of whisky.

It was as though the pain in my arm and the fumes in my head were fighting for mastery. Dimly, I realised whisky was the only pain-killer I had available. I drank more of it, swallowed more aspirins. I drifted off into a kinda soggy doze, opened my eyes from time to time when the pain pulled me out of my sleep. Some time during that nightmarish doze, she came out of the bathroom, climbed into bed and turned off the light. I reached for the bottle, drank more whisky and gritted my teeth against the pain, waiting for the numbing effects of the spirit to enable me to sleep.

Dawn was breaking when a rending hot stab of pain that would not be subdued aroused me. I got up, paced up and down the room in a kinda pained coma. After a time, it subsided. I found I was sweating and weak. I examined my arm, found the yellow spot had grown to the size of a sixpence. Then I felt under my armpit, and there was a large lump there. The poison was running through me, getting into the bloodstream.

Wild fears beat at me. It might mean having my arm amputated. It might even mean I'd die. I reached for the whisky bottle, found it empty, put it back unsteadily on the table, so that it fell. The noise awoke her.

She sat up in bed, stared at me anxiously. "What's the matter, Lee?"

"Aw, leave me alone, will ya?

"You're ill," she said. She sounded worried.

"Gotta bit of trouble," I gritted.

"It's your arm," she said. "Let me look at it."

I moved towards her, she climbed out of bed, came as far as her chain would permit. Her forehead was crinkled in sympathy as she drew in a pained breath. "Gee, that's bad," she said. "That's real bad. You'll have to go to hospital right away."

"That's out," I said flatly.

"But you'll have to go," she protested. "That's really dangerous. Anything could happen."

I grinned mirthlessly. "Sure. Anything could happen!" I got another bottle of whisky from the cabinet. I cleared a small table, laid out a clean towel, bandages, a razor blade and a pair of pliers. I put a kettle on to boil, and while it was boiling poured whisky into a cup, dropped in the razor blade, the pliers. I applied a match to the pliers, held them while a blue flame hovered around them.

She was watching me all the time. Finally she said, disbelievingly: "You're not going to do it yourself!"

I wasn't looking forward to it. It didn't help having her so critical. "Sure I'm doing it myself."

"You're crazy," she whispered. "You're running all kinds of risks."

"Leave me alone, will ya, lady? It's my arm. Not yours."

The water was boiling. I filled the basin, put more water on the stove. She was watching me all the time with wide, anxious eyes. "Why don't you go to hospital?"

I ignored her, balanced a mirror so I could see my arm. It was gonna be awkward. I'd have to work with my left hand, probe for the piece of needle with blunt pliers, unable to see what I was doing.

"You really intend to go through with this?"

"D'you think I wanna lose my arm?"

"You're crazy," she said. "You can't do it yourself."

"I'll have a damned good try."

There was a long pause. She said, slowly: "You'd better let me do it."

I turned and stared at her. It was the right answer. I'd make a mess of it myself. I licked my lips. "D'you know what you're taking on?"

Her face was set and determined. "You can't do it yourself," she said. "Let me do it."

I turned away from her. "Forget it," I grunted. "I can handle it." It was gonna be messy. It was better to keep her out of it.

Her voice was low and contemptuous. "You're afraid of me. You're afraid I'll take advantage when you're ill. It's your own weakness. You can't trust yourself, so you can't trust anyone else."

I turned back to her, stared at her levelly. She glared back, and suddenly I wanted to make her crack, make her lose her confidence. Without another word, I carried the table across to her, placed it beside the bed. The kettle was boiling again. I brought that over too, more water to clean up the mess.

Her lips trembled slightly. "What do I do?"

"Cut and probe," I said brutally. "The needle's in there, deep down, maybe a quarter of an inch down. You cut with the razor, probe with the pliers, draw it out."

Her face was white, scared. "Is this all I have to do it with?"

I smiled grimly. "What d'you want? A surgery?"

It wasn't pleasant for me. You might think I was being brave. The truth was, I was suffering such agony, I was willing to endure anything that might relieve me of pain.

She looked at the razor lying in the cup of whisky. She looked at the sterilized pliers and the bowl of steaming water. She shuddered.

"Forget it," I said. "I'll take care of it."

She caught her breath, grabbed at me. "No," she said quickly. "You can't do it yourself. I'll do it."

I sat on the edge of the bed, rolled up my shirt-sleeve.

She took towels, spread them on the bed. "Lie down," she instructed. "Make yourself as comfortable as possible."

I lay down as she wanted, watched her all the time. Revulsion was written on her face. But she mastered herself, placed more towels underneath my arm, surrounded it with cotton-wool. She poured whisky on cotton-wool, dabbed it gently on my arm. I winced. "I'll have a shot out the bottle," I told her.

She held the bottle for me. I took three deep gulps, big gulps that caused the whisky to burn into my belly, my eyes to water with the sharp bite of it.

Now she'd started, she seemed more confident. She pulled the table close so it would be convenient, took the razor blade from the cup and held it between her fingers. It was a plain blade, difficult to cut with.

She sat with the razor poised, looked at me anxiously. "How d'you feel?"

"Lousy," I said. "But go ahead, just the same."

"You're ready?"

"Sure," I said. "Just you start, don't waste time. Do it quickly."

"I'm going to cut first. Just one cut, long and deep. Are you ready?"

"Sure," I panted. "Go ahead."

"Don't watch," she instructed. "Shut your eyes. It'll be easier that way."

I did what she said, shut my eyes. I felt her cool fingers encircle my arm, holding it firmly. I let my body go limp, waiting for the sharp, sudden slash. In the same moment, I realized I'd played right into her hands. She could slash at my throat or at my pulse. I'd played right into her hands and ...

The pain was in my arm, sharp sweet pain, cutting deep and with agonizing slowness. It was as though my swollen arm exploded, and the sharp, cutting pain gave me blessed relief when bursting, throbbing pressure was released.

I opened my eyes, saw her reddened fingers desperately pressing together the raw lips of the deep gash, trying to stem the sharp spurt of blood. There was panic in her blue eyes as she pressed the wound, trying to keep it closed. There was blood on her cheeks and a great red splash on her shoulder, trickling down to her white breasts. The blood musta spurted like a fountain when she cut.

There was cold sweat on my forehead, and there was pain. Hell there was pain. But it was sharp and piercing, not burning and throbbing. And I didn't feel that it was part of my body. It was an arm with which I had no connection, a limb that was that of a stranger.

"Whisky," I said thickly. "Saturate it. Don't worry about the blood. Start probing."

As soon as her fingers released the wound, it began to bleed furiously. Hot blood flowed down my arm, dripped from my fingertips. Then she was back with the whisky, sponging with cotton-wool, pouring raw spirits into the lips of the wound. I almost rolled off the bed with the sharp burn of it. My feet drummed on the bed and the fingers of my good arm clutched a thick blanket, tore it.

The whisky stopped a lotta the bleeding. She was biting her lip now, her eyes pained by the horror of what she was doing.

"Probe for it," I rasped. "Get it out."

She fumbled with the pliers, dropped them twice before she got a grip on them. She'd taken so long, the wound had filled with blood again. I pushed her hand away from my arm. "Whisky," I said tersely.

She held the bottle poised. With my finger and thumb I deliberately pulled the wound open as she tilted the bottle. The raw spirits ran deep into the wound, so that once again I wanted to drum my feet. "Quick," I rasped faintly. "Can you see it?"

She peered. "No," she said weakly.

"Feel for it then."

Her eyes were fluttery. But she probed with her little finger. "I've got it," she said.

"Can you reach it?"
"I'll have to ... cut some more."
"Jeepers," I yelled aloud. "This isn't a picnic. Snap it up, will ya?"
This time I felt her cutting. Every primitive instinct inside me urged me to wrench away. But I managed to remain still enough for her. I had my head turned from her, my teeth biting into my forearm.
"I can see it," she said.
I didn't say anything. If I'd spoken, it would have broken my self-control.
"I'm going to get it now."
The blunt nose of the pliers was gentle after the cutting blade of the razor. I felt them probing, seemed to hear them grate on the tip of the needle, and then it felt like the bone was being sucked out of my arm.
"I've got it," she said. Her voice was faint, like she was gonna keel over.
Without turning to look at her, I said weakly: "I'll be okay ... in a minute."
Again the sharp sting of spirits in a raw wound, then she was pressing my arm, squeezing the wound so it hurt all over again.
I wrenched my head around to her, my jaws parted with pain. "What the hell ...?"
"It's the poison," she said. "I've got to get it out. I've gotta clean it up."
The needle had been festering, threatening blood-poisoning. The wound had to be thoroughly cleaned and disinfected. Somewhere I found the strength to hold on to my consciousness while she probed, squeezed and swabbed.
"I think it's okay now," she said.
It made me sick to look at it. A deep gash in my arm, so deep it musta been nearly through to the bone. She cut sticking plaster into lengths, pulled the edges of the wound together and fastened it that way with sticking plaster.
She did it like she was in a dream. When the last piece of plaster had been smoothed into place, she keeled over.
She was kneeling down, so hadn't far to fall. She went over sideways, and her head hit the carpet with a bang. I felt

faint and dizzy. I sat up on the edge of the bed, pushed myself to a standing position and got another bottle of whisky, forced the neck of the bottle between her teeth. It wasn't surprising she'd fainted. The room was a shambles. Her arms were slippery to the shoulders with my blood, and it had stained her underclothing too. The carpet was littered with blood-stained swabs of cotton-wool. On the table, still adhering to the blood-stained pliers, was the cause of the trouble, an inch-long piece of broken needle, discoloured and poisonous-looking.

She didn't come around until I'd cleaned away the swabs, removed the blood-soaked towels from the bed, and with some difficulty lifted her on to it. Her eyes fluttered. She looked up into my face. "Tell me ... you're all right?" she asked.

I was hazy, weak as a kitten and feeling I was gonna vomit. "Sure," I said. "I'm okay now."

She worked up a smile. "I'm sorry I had to hurt you."

"That's okay," I said gruffly. She made a movement like she was gonna get off the bed. "Take it easy," I said. "There ain't no hurry."

"Gotta clean up."

"That's okay. I've taken care of it. Most of it anyway."

She looked down at her blood-stained arms. She shuddered. "I'd better wash."

I pushed her back on the pillows. "No hurry," I said. "Take it easy."

Her blue eyes smiled up into mine. "All right, Lee," she said obediently. She closed her eyes, relaxed.

I got more hot water, pulled the table over beside her and washed the blood off her arms. She did the rest of it herself, discreetly lowered the bodice, washed her breasts quickly, shooting me shy little glances from time to time as though to figure out whether I was watching her lustfully or disinterestedly.

I was feeling better already. The smart of the wound was still keen. But it was a healthy kinda pain. The relief from that intolerable throbbing was like finding myself alive again. I said gruffly but sincerely, "I sure am grateful for what you've done. It took a lotta nerve, and maybe it's saved my arm."

"Something had to be done," she said simply. "I just had to help."

"I'm grateful," I said awkwardly. I hesitated. "If there's anything I can do for you ..." My voice trailed off. I knew what she would want. She'd want me to release her. She'd give me her promise she wouldn't go to the cops. And that would put me in one helluva spot. Because I'd made up my mind she wasn't gonna get loose from me until I was good and ready.

"There is one thing you can do for me," she said quickly.

My mouth was dry. I was gonna be awful ungrateful after what she had done. "Yeah? What d'you want?"

"My handbag," she said. "Get my handbag from the car, will you?" Her hand instinctively went towards her hair, fluffed it. "I feel simply terrible, Lee. I haven't combed my hair and ..." She dropped her eyes shyly. "Well, you know how it is, girls always like to have their make-up handy."

I got up slowly, relieved at the simpleness of the request. "Sure," I said. "I'll get your handbag. I'll get it for you now."

CHAPTER TWELVE

It was four days before I was ready to make my next move. My arm was healing rapidly, as good as new. And as was to be expected, Helen had become more and more disgruntled every day as her confinement became more and more wearing. She pleaded again and again to be released, promised she'd do anything she could to help me. She grumbled about the food, complained the chain was rubbing her raw, finally sank into a gloomy, sullen silence, refusing even to exchange monosyllables.

The police were way off track. The FBI were investigating a report that Helen's car had been seen in the Middle West. Police investigation into the kidnapping had left Cleveland, was spreading throughout the rest of the country. There was no fresh news about Manton.

I'd figured a way to connect with Frisk. I went downtown, made discreet enquiries. I had more success than Manton. He hadn't been able to find his daughter, had accused Frisk of hiding her away. But she'd turned up at the inquest, had fainted and got herself a certain amount of publicity. A few well-distributed bucks among reporters got me her address over on the North side of town. It was a discreet block of flats in a good-class neighbourhood. Her flat was on the first floor. I pressed the bell half-a-dozen times and knocked half-a-dozen times. It didn't get me anywhere. I went downstairs to the hall-porter, asked about her.

"She's up there, fella," he said. "That dame never goes out." He looked at me curiously. "She ain't sociable," he said. "Don't have many visitors."

I slipped him a buck to silence his curiosity, went upstairs and rang the bell again. This time, I kept my thumb on the bell, determined to wait until the battery ran out or she opened up.

She opened up. She stood in the doorway, swaying slightly and her glassy eyes staring at me uncomprehendingly.

"Jessica Manton?"

"Who're you? What d'you want?" She slurred her words badly.

She was probably twenty-four or twenty-five. But she looked older. Much older. That was on account of the deathly whiteness of her face and the worn expression in her eyes. Her black hair was dishevelled and dirty, falling untidily across her forehead. She wore a grubby, crumpled silk blouse that was open to the waist, a crumpled green slip stained with spilt wine, and one stocking hung around her ankle. The other stocking was wrinkled and twisted. The smell of gin was heavy on her breath.

"I wanna have a talk about your father," I said.

Her eyes widened and then narrowed. She pressed her weight against the door, began to close it in my face. "Scram," she slurred. "Get outta here. I doan wanna talk."

I pushed against her, got the door wide enough to slip through inside. Her weight slammed the door. That left her and me on the inside. She stared around at me dazedly, like she didn't understand how I came to be there.

"I wanna talk, Jessica," I said.

She bleared at me, pushed her hair back from her forehead and scratched herself through her slip, high up on the inside of the thigh. "Who're you, anyway?" She swayed slightly.

"Get me a drink, huh?" I said. "Then we'll talk."

"Drink?" She crinkled her forehead. Then her eyes brightened. "Yeah, less'av a drin'."

She shuffled along the corridor in her stockinged feet, swaying unsteadily. It led to her bedroom. At least, I guess she called it her bedroom. The windows were jammed tight, the atmosphere thick and unbreatheable, like the room had been lived in for many days. It probably had. The bed was rumpled disorder. She'd probably been lying there when I first rang. There was a half-filled gin bottle beside the bed, and other empty bottles lying around. Her clothes were lying around, too, dropped on the floor as she'd stripped them off.

She sat on the edge of the bed, reached for the gin bottle and sloshed it into a glass like it was water. She drank half of it before she remembered me. She held the bottle towards me. "Hey you. Help yourself."

I found a glass on the sideboard. I smelt it, could tell it had been used. I poured myself a small shot, studied Jessica while I was doing it. She was a pretty dame. But right now she was drugged with liquor. Her stained slip rucked up as she sat on the edge of the bed, and she neither seemed to know or care that I was there. I'd have had to be blind not to know she wasn't wearing step-ins.

"I wanna talk a little while, Jessica," I said gently.

She stared across at me, scowled. Her eyes were a million miles away. "I don't wanna talk," she said thickly.

"When did you last see Frisk?" I shot at her suddenly.

It was instinctive to her. Her eyes flicked across the room, rested on a small cabinet. Then her eyes flickered back to mine, cunning and crafty. "When's he coming?" she asked eagerly. "He'll have to came soon. He knows that, doesn't he? He'll have to come soon."

"He's afraid to come," I said slowly. "He killed your father. He shot him."

Her eyes were suddenly terrified. "What d'you mean, he may not come? He's got to come." Her eyes were wide with desperation. She shouted at me: "He's got to come. He's got to come soon."

"Sure, sure," I said. "He'll be coming. But did you hear what I said? He killed your father."

"He killed my father," she repeated dumbly. Her eyes flicked away from mine, stared at the carpet. "He killed my father," she repeated. But her voice was toneless, as though her words had no meaning.

It was terrible a young girl like her should be so fuddled with drink. "When did you last see Frisk?" I asked gently. "How often do you see him?"

Once again when I mentioned his name, her eyes flicked to that little cabinet. Then her eyes were back on mine again, crafty and cunning. "When is he coming?" she asked eagerly. "He's gotta come soon."

"Sure," I said. "He'll come soon." At the same time, I drifted a coupla paces towards that cabinet. She took another gulp at her drink, finished it off. Mechanically, she scratched at the inside of her thigh. This time, she pulled up her slip to do it. It was then I saw the rash of pinpricks, red and ugly against her white skin. It was then I remembered the hypodermic Gunn so conveniently had at hand, and it was then that I crossed the room swiftly, tugged at the drawer of the cabinet.

It was locked.

She landed on my shoulders just a second later, knees gripping my waist and hands tearing at my hair so I went over backwards, surprised by the suddenness of her attack.

She rolled from underneath, clung to my arm and tried to gnaw my hand off. I jerked free, thrust at her so she went over backwards, sprawling on her hereafter. I'd climbed to my knees by the time she launched herself at me again, bearing me sideways on to the carpet. Then she was sitting half on my chest and half on my neck, tugging at my hair with one hand, trying to gouge my eyes with the other.

I grabbed her wrists, had my work cut out hanging on to them. I tried to squirm away from beneath her. But the full weight of her body was pinning me down, her eyes wild and crazy. For a moment, it seemed like a deadlock. She couldn't blind me and I couldn't squirm her weight from off my chest and neck. Then she got a new idea, clamped her thighs together, tried to suffocate me.

I had an answer to that. Not a pleasant one. I moved my head, dug my teeth deep into hot, burning flesh.

That shifted her!

She got off me like I was red hot. She shrieked with the pain of it, and in mad fury tried to kick in my ribs. She hurt her toes more than she hurt me. Then she was wrapping herself around me again, tearing with her nails, butting with her head and using her teeth whenever she got a chance.

I had a pretty good idea what was in that cabinet. It was her dope supply. That's what Frisk had made of her, a dope addict. He'd probably met her when she was an impressionable age, introduced her to dope, gradually built her up so she was dependent on it and dependent on him giving it her.

Dope had become precious to her. It had become life itself. She would fight to defend it as a man would fight to defend his life.

But she'd been drinking, too. And a combination of both of them had turned her into a drunken slut. A dame content to lie around the house all day, alternately drinking and giving herself shots so she remained perpetually in a twilight world. That suited Frisk. She was a dame, ready and waiting, willing whenever he wanted her, because of the supply of life-giving stimulant he brought with him. But he was killing the dame. Three or four years more at most and she'd be a nervous wreck, jittery and ready for the asylum.

Yet this girl could be valuable to me. I could use her to trap Frisk. I could use her, that is, provided I could make her understand. The way she was fighting me, struggling ferociously as I held her down and away from me, it didn't seem like she was gonna be reasonable.

I had her at a real disadvantage now, face down on the bed with her arms twisted up behind her. She couldn't do much except harmlessly kick her legs.

"Listen, Jessica," I said gently. "I wanna talk with you. I wanna talk seriously."

"You're trying to rob me," she shrieked. "You're a thief. You're trying to take it from me."

"I don't want to do anything of the sort," I protested gently.

"They sent you," she said. "They're always after me. Trying to take it away from me. You're one of them."

I wasn't sure if it was the booze talking or the drug. It could have been both. But if it was the gin talking, there was one good way I knew to sober her down.

She didn't come willingly. She struggled every inch of the way. I found the bathroom, put the plug in the bath, turned on the cold water shower and the bath tap at the same time. She was struggling all the time, and it was hard work holding her. When the bath was almost full, I edged her over to it. Maybe she didn't know what I had in mind. Maybe she didn't even understand what was happening. She still kept struggling. I chose my moment, waited until the backs of her thighs were against the edge of the bath, and pushed gently, holding her so she wouldn't fall too heavily.

She went in neatly, arms clawing frantically to save herself as she went down. The water parted beneath her weight, rushed in over the top of her, flooded over the edge of the bath. Her head emerged from the water, and she was spouting water like a porpoise as she grappled for the sides of the bath.

I was getting wet myself, but I didn't mind. I stood at the head of the bath, pushed her head under the water each time she came up. And that water sure was cold. She was puffing and spluttering, and her face was going blue now. Each time she came up, I gave her a few seconds to get her breath before I pushed her under again.

I kept her in that bath for maybe ten minutes. Ten minutes is a long time to be completely submerged in icy water. At the end of that time, she hadn't any fight left in her, barely enough strength to climb out of the bath.

I left her weakly clambering over the edge of the bath, looking like a half-drowned rat. I locked the bathroom door from the outside, so she couldn't get loose, and went back to the bedroom. I used a penknife to break open the cabinet drawer. Inside was a hypodermic and six cellulose capsules containing a colourless liquid. I left the hypodermic, put the capsules in my pocket. Then I went back to the bathroom.

She hadn't made any attempt to follow me. She'd spent the time stripping off her wet clothes. Now she was completely naked, trying to dry herself and rub warmth into her cold body.

She glared at me viciously, spoke through pale lips and chattering teeth. "What the hell d'ya do that for?"

"I wanted to talk," I said. "You'd had a skinful, needed sobering up."

Her eyes narrowed. "What's it to you if I'm sober or not?" She hadn't any modesty, made no attempt to use the towel discreetly. Her thighs wasn't the only place she'd used that hypodermic. There was another rash of pinpricks on each arm and on her belly. I sighed wearily. "I told you a while back that Frisk killed your father," I said. "It didn't seem to mean anything to you. Does it now you're sober?"

Her eyes were hard. "What d'you mean? Frisk killed my father?"

"He shot him," I said. "Put two bullets in his chest. Then he tried to frame the murder on somebody else."

Her eyes were still hard. It was as though shutters came down over them. "What if he did?" she said tonelessly. "What can I do about it?"

"Depends," I said. "What do you want to do about it?"

"Just leave me alone," she said wearily. "Just leave me alone."

She pushed past me, stark naked, padded on bare feet back to the bedroom. I followed her leisurely; she'd gone straight to the cabinet, knew I'd taken the capsules. There were two high spots burning high up on her cheeks. She held out her hand, and her lips were trembling. "Give it to me," she said fiercely. "Give it to me. Let me have it. You can't take it from me."

"I'm gonna let you have it," I said. "Don't work yourself up. But you've gotta do me a little favour first."

"Anything," she said breathlessly. "Anything you say." Her eyes were pleading now, her hands extended towards me. Maybe it wasn't exactly a romantic moment, but it was certainly a confusing one. I could never have doubted she was a woman.

I cleared my throat awkwardly. "Wouldn't it be better if you ... er ... put something on? Huh?"

"You've gotta give it to me," she said fiercely.

"Sure, sure," I said soothingly. "I'm gonna give it to you. You can have it all back within an hour. But you've gotta take a little trip with me first."

"I want it now," she said urgently. "I've gotta have a shot now." Her eyes looked towards the clock. "I've gotta have a shot now. It's getting late."

"Do what I want, and you'll get it," I told her.

Her eyes were panic-stricken. "You don't understand," she said. "I can't leave it an hour. It'll drive me crazy. I've gotta have it to keep me steady."

I thought it over. It wouldn't be smart to take her with me, find her crack up halfway. A hophead is liable to do anything when they crack. "I'll make a deal," I said quickly. "You can take a shot now. Don't overdo it. After you've done what I want, I'll give you the others."

"Sure, sure," she said eagerly. "I'll do anything. But I've got to have a shot now."

I wasn't familiar with drugs. I didn't know what the dose was. If she took too much, she was liable to fold up on me, go off into a drugged sleep. On the other hand, the right amount would keep her level, stop her from blowing her top.

"Do what I say," I said. "Stand away from that cabinet."

She stood away from the cabinet. I got out the hypodermic, took one of the capsules from my pocket and nipped off the end. She watched with eager glistening eyes as I squirted about a quarter of the contents of the capsule into the hypodermic chamber.

She was watching me all the time, her eyes gauging and measuring, calculating and anxious. "But what about ...?" she began.

I held up the hypodermic. "That's all you're gonna get," I said grimly.

"But what about ...?" she began again.

I pointed the capsule towards the carpet, crushed it between my thumb and finger so that a thin spray spurted across the floor. She gave a shriek of wild frenzy, threw herself down on the carpet, rubbed her fingers on the damp patches like she was trying to pick it up. I let the empty capsule drop from my fingers, ground it beneath my heel. She looked up at me with wild, pleading in her eyes. "Why did you do that?" she screamed. "Why did you do it?"

I held the hypodermic towards her. "You can have your shot," I said. "You get the other capsules later."

She wasn't taking a chance on missing the little that was in the hypodermic. She snatched it from my hand like she'd had plenty of practice, her thumb on the plunger and the needle poised. She inspected herself carefully, decided on the right hip. She rested her right foot on a chair, gathered up a pucker of flesh between finger and thumb and, with a swift, experienced stab, drove the needle under her skin. She took a deep breath that sounded like a gasp of pleasurable anticipation, pressed down the plunger very carefully and slowly, like it was giving her exquisite pleasure and she wanted to prolong it.

"How long you been doing this?" I asked.

Her eyes lifted, inspected me sullenly. "What's it to you?"

I shrugged my shoulders. "Just seems a crazy kinda habit to me."

She carefully dismantled the hypodermic, unscrewed the needle. "What do I have to do to get the other?" she asked sullenly.

"I told you. We're gonna take a little trip. It'll be all over in an hour."

"It'd better be," she said. She crossed the room, opened up an untidy wardrobe. None of the dresses was on hangers, all hanging untidily from hooks or dropped carelessly on the floor of the wardrobe. She picked up the nearest one to hand, a green silk dress.

"How much does Frisk give you?" I asked.

"What's it to you?"

"Just a casual enquiry."

"He don't give me nothing," she sneered. "Just my supply. Pays the rent, of course."

"Is it worth it?"

She worked her arms into the dress, pulled it over her shoulders, down around her waist. It was silk, clinging, and didn't reach quite to her knees. When it was buttoned, the way her breasts rolled beneath the silk, showed the dress was all she was wearing. "Look, fella," she asked "D'you know some place I can get some money and some other place I can buy dope? That's one way I can get square with Frisk. He started me on this. Now I can't shake free from it."

"You could go to hospital, offer yourself for treatment."

She laughed at me. "D'you think I'm that crazy? D'you know what they do? They feed you the dope in little pieces. You go crazy, dying for it. They don't cure you, they just make you suffer."

She'd found two shoes now, pushed her feet into them. She looked around, found her handbag, carefully placed in it the hypodermic and the needle.

"What's that for?"

"I want that next shot just so soon as I can get it."

"We won't be more than an hour."

Her eyes gleamed, her white teeth glistened. "That's right," she said. "Won't be more than an hour."

I could tell what she was thinking. She was gonna come back here, needle herself, lie on the bed and drift off into that twilight dreamworld of hers.

"I'm ready," she said.

I looked at the green dress. I cleared my throat. I said, meaningfully: "You sure you feel safe?"

She stared at me in surprise. Then she understood. She shrugged her shoulders. "Well, if it makes you feel any happier."

She dug down in the wardrobe again, came up with a pair of briefs. She was completely uninhibited. She climbed into them right there in front of me.

"Where you taking me?" she asked, as she pulled them on, wrestled them firmly into position.

I swallowed, flushed and said hoarsely: "You'll find out. You'll find out."

"And we won't be more than an hour," she said anxiously. "You promise." She smoothed her frock.

"No longer," I said huskily. "Let's go."

CHAPTER THIRTEEN

I took her back to my house. Crossing town, the traffic was thick, and it took more than three-quarters of an hour. When I pulled up outside the front door, she looked around her apprehensively. "Say, fella. You ain't trying to pull something?"

"What are you scared of?"

There was that desperate note in her voice. "You've gotta play square with me. You've gotta let me have it the way you promised."

"Sure, sure," I said. "You'll get it. Just do what I tell you."

She was getting nervous now. When I slammed the door behind us, it echoed through the empty house. She jumped, stared around like she was afraid little green men were gonna spring out on her.

"This way," I grunted, led the way up the stairs. She followed, hesitantly and with obvious suspicion. But I had dope in my pocket. She was more scared of losing that than anything else.

I ushered her into the room, and Helen, who was sitting on the bed reading a magazine, looked up sharply and then narrowed her eyes. I could sense the relief in Jessica when she realized there was another dame in the house. But it took her only a few seconds to realize the significance of the chain around Helen's waist. She spun around to face me, backed a coupla paces.

By this time, I'd closed the door behind me. I leaned my shoulders against the panels.

There was wild apprehension in her eyes. "Look, fella," she said in a frightened voice. "You ain't gonna start anything. I'd rather be with Frisk. He's on the level, gives me my stuff regularly." She backed another coupla paces.

"You ain't got a thing to worry about," I said wearily. "You've just gotta make a telephone call for me. After that, you get what you want."

"Who is she?" asked Helen.

"Manton's daughter."

Jessica interjected: "What d'you want me to do, fella? Let's get it over with."

"You've gotta make a telephone call," I told her. "You've gotta say it just the way I tell you."

"What are we waiting for?"

"You've gotta do it just right," I said. "You've gotta make it sound convincing. You've gotta say the right things, too. I'll write it down for you."

I wrote down what she had to say. I made her repeat it again and again until she knew it off by heart. Then she had to practice to get the right tone into her voice. I wasn't taking any chances. I wanted everything to go off smoothly. That's why it took her almost an hour to get it just the way I wanted it. By that time, her hands were shaking and her eyes getting out of focus.

"You've gotta let me have another shot, fella," she pleaded. "Just so I can do it right."

Visibly she was in need of another small jolt. She'd go to pieces without it. I took another capsule from my pocket. "Give me that needle."

She gave it to me with anxious, trembling fingers. Her fingers trembled so eagerly, she wasn't even able to screw the needle into the hypodermic.

I allowed her a quarter of a capsule. She watched with shining eyes when I squirted it into the hypodermic chamber. Then she gave a frantic squeal when she realized it was gonna be just a small jolt. She tackled me then, tried to wrestle the capsule from my hand. I wrenched away her clutching fingers, held the hypodermic high, poised like I was going to smash it against the wall. She froze, horrified.

"Gonna cut it out?" I rasped.

"Let me have it, fella," she pleaded. "Let me have it, will ya?"

"That's all you get for now," I told her. "You'll get the other later, when you've done what I want."

She was cowed, almost whimpering. When I lowered my hand, held it towards her, she snatched at the hypodermic like a little dog snatching a bone from a Great Dane.

Helen, who'd been watching with wide eyes, asked: "Lee! You're surely not going to let her ..." Her voice trailed off as she watched Jessica.

With frantic haste, Jessica put one foot on a chair, pulled up her skirt, exposing the rash of pinpricks on the inside of her thigh. High up, she pinched a fold of flesh between finger and thumb. The hand holding the hypodermic was trembling so badly she seemed to jab too deeply. But there was no sign of pain on her face; instead, an expression of serene happiness as she slowly pressed home the plunger, prolonging as long as possible the sensation of the dope flooding into her body.

Helen's eyes were wide and pained. "You shouldn't let her, Lee. You'll make her worse."

Jessica glared at her, moistened her forefinger with her tongue, rubbed away the tiny bead of blood that showed on her thigh, and carefully wiped the needle.

"How d'ya feel now?" I asked.

"Just what I wanted." She looked around. "Got a drink?"

"We'll get this job done first," I said grimly. "Let's hear you say your piece once more. Then you can make the call."

It was Frisk she telephoned. She held the receiver away from her ear so I could listen to him.

"What the hell d'you mean by telephoning me?" he demanded.

"Getting short," she told him. "You've gotta let me have some more. Quick."

He was irritable. "I'm coming tomorrow. I never miss. You know that. And don't ring me again."

"I've gotta see you before that," she said tensely.

"Forget it. I'm busy."

She got a warning note into her voice. "You'd better meet me," she said. "I know something!"

The meaning in her voice got him worried. "What are you talking about?"

"About my father's death," she said. "You killed him. I know that now. And I can prove it, too."

There was a long, frightened silence. Then he said, hoarsely: "You've had too much dope. Maybe I didn't ought to bring you any more."

"You can't scare me that way," she told him. "Because I've got too much on you. I can prove you killed my father."

"So you've got a crazy idea," he mocked. "What d'you want me to do about it?"

"Meet me tonight," she said. "And bring some more dope."

There was another silence. You could almost hear his thoughts whirling and planning. "Okay," he said. "Where d'you want me to meet you?"

"Nine o'clock. Corner of Madison and Palm Tree Avenue. Come in your car."

He gave a deep sigh. "Okay, Jessica," he said. "I'll be there. I'll knock whatever crazy ideas you've got out out of your head."

"You'll bring the dope?"

"Sure," he said. "I'll bring some."

"One other thing," she said quietly, meaningfully.

"Well?"

"Come alone," she told him. "And I mean it. Come alone. Because I know exactly how you killed my father. I've got it all written down. I can prove it, too, and you'll swing for it if necessary. So come alone. And if there's anyone with you or watching you, don't expect to meet me, because I'll go straight to the cops."

"What are you talking about?" he demanded. But he was scared. You could tell it in his voice. "You gone crazy or something?"

"I don't wanna risk anything," she told him. "I don't wanna be found dead in a ditch, taken to the morgue with a label tied to my toe."

This time the silence was longer. You could tell Frisk was shaken. His voice was a croak when he said: "Okay, then. I'll see you. I'll come alone."

"You'd better," she said, before she hung up.

"That's fine," I told her. "You did that swell."

She scratched the inside of her thigh, looked at me hopefully. "Do I get it now?"

I looked at my watch. It was five o'clock. "You'll have to wait a bit, sister," I told her.

Her eyes filled with anger and there was a tinge of apprehension in them too. "What do you mean?" she asked desperately, panting.

"You're my insurance," I said. "You've gotta stick around until we know Frisk is gonna turn up."

Her lips trembled. "You can't keep me without it all that time."

I pushed past her. "Don't worry," I said. "You'll get your dope. I'll keep you going."

She was around in front of me, clutching at my arm. "But it's no good like that," she pleaded. "It's not the same. I've gotta have a dose, a full dose. You've gotta let me have it, fella, or I'll go crazy."

I figured it out. A quarter of a capsule had kept her going for over an hour. If I let her have the rest of the capsule, it should keep her happy until just about nine o'clock. If Frisk didn't keep the appointment, she'd still be hanging around, knowing I had the rest of her capsules.

"I'll do anything you say," she pleaded. "I'll stick around if you want. But just let me have a jolt, will ya?"

I let her have the rest of the capsule. It almost filled the hypodermic. Helen and I watched with hard eyes as she settled herself comfortably in a chair, pulled up her skirt. It was her left hip this time, and a much bigger jolt. You could see her body relaxing pleasurably as she pushed down on the plunger. "How about a drink, fella?" she asked. "That'll just about make it right."

I got her a drink. Just one wouldn't hurt her, I figured. I took it to her. She lay back in the chair, completely relaxed like her body had turned to jelly. There was a woozy, dream-like expression on her face, her legs were ungracefully parted and the hem of her dress was still up around her waist. That dreamy look became suddenly inviting when she took the glass. "I feel good, fella," she said.

"Glad you're happy," I said grimly.

She chuckled. A throaty, sexy chuckle. "You wanna be nice to me, huh?" Her hand reached for mine, pulling and guiding it as she closed her eyes happily.

I gently disengaged my hand, and she pouted. But she didn't open her eyes. The expression of stupefied happiness on her face showed she was already entering her own private twilight world, the world of a drug addict, in which for a short span of time dreams become reality, when sensory emotions of all kinds become satisfied.

"Feel sleepy?" I asked.

She gave a little sigh of contentment, finished her drink at one gulp, still without opening her eyes, and then let the glass drop on the carpet. She gave a little murmur of contentment, snuggled down into the armchair like she was snuggling deliciously in the arms of her lover.

Helen said in an awed voice: "It takes effect quickly, doesn't it?"

"Yeah," I said drily. I was suddenly embarrassed, a Peeping Tom, spying on somebody's privacy. Anger began to smoulder deep down inside me. Because Jessica was one more wrecked life that could be laid to Frisk's account. Yeah, it was typical of him. Ingratiate himself with a nice young dame, introduce her to dope until she became an addict, and then hold up her supplies until she'd do anything to get them.

The Jessica I saw now was a travesty of what she could have been. She'd lost her will-power, all initiative and her interest in life. Always she was scheming to escape to her narcotic twilight world. But there was still plenty of evidence she'd have been quite a dame. She had good looks, she had nice legs too. They were slender and shapely so I didn't mind looking at them. But the way she was slumped in the chair with her legs parted widely showed that ugly rash on the inside of her thighs. I bent over her, gently pulled down the hem of her skirt.

Her warm lips were parted, showing white, glistening teeth. She was breathing quickly, and there was a stupidly sensuous smile on her face. Her lips pouted slightly when I pulled down her skirt. She pulled it up again – brazenly! She wasn't asleep and she wasn't conscious. She neither knew we were there or cared. Her sensuous twilight world was all she knew or wanted, and she wouldn't awaken from it until the effect of the drug had worn away.

I turned away from her quickly, embarrassed by her sensuous dreaming. Helen said, reproachfully: "Giving it to her is helping to kill her, helping to drive her crazy."

"What could I do?" I asked gruffly. "She's needling herself every day as it is. Can you blame me for making use of it?"

Her eyes flashed. "I certainly do. If you had any sense of decency, you'd have the girl taken to hospital, have her cured."

"I want Frisk," I said grimly. "I want Frisk more than I want anything else. And I'm going to get him." I went across the room, put the spare capsules I'd taken from Jessica in a drawer of a cabinet, and then made some coffee.

I gave a cup to Helen. She sat cross-legged on the bed, sipped it slowly.

"Cigarette?" I asked.

"I'd like one, please."

We smoked in silence for a while. Then she asked, abruptly: "You're going to meet Frisk?"

"Clever of you to figure that," I mocked.

"Supposin' ... supposin' there's trouble?"

"There will be," I said grimly.

"I mean ... supposin' you get in trouble?"

"That's a risk I've got to take."

"But if you weren't as clever as you thought – can't you see what I'm trying to say, Lee? If anything should happen to you, I'll be chained up here. Nobody will know anything about it."

"That will be tough."

Her blue eyes were soft and pleading. "Why don't you believe me, Lee? Release me. I'll never tell anybody about you or what I saw. Why don't you believe me?"

I looked at her steadily. "I do believe you."

"Then you'll let me go ...?" she asked eagerly.

I shook my head slowly. "I'm not taking any chances. Frisk is the guy I'm after. Once I've got him, I'll take all the chances in the world."

Her eyes were moist. "Can't you realize what hell it is for me, Lee? I've been here days now. It's killing me. I can walk just a coupla paces each way and then lie on the bed. That's all. Nothing else. It's driving me crazy. And this chain is driving me crazy too."

"It won't be for long," I said consolingly. "If I let you loose, you'll take a powder the moment I take my eyes off you."

She sat on the edge of the bed, pulling at the chain with her fingers. "It's rubbing me raw, Lee," she complained. "Look what it's doing to me."

I crossed to her, prepared for any smart move she might try. The garment she wore was so fragile it had torn away beneath the rub of the chain. The skin beneath was reddened and chafed, her waist encircled by a red impression of the steel chain. "It's driving me mad, Lee," she complained. "It's always there. When I sleep at night, I have to keep changing positions because it's hurting me. When I move around, it's catching at me, always with me."

Her blue eyes were looking up into my face soulfully. It wasn't just the ridge around her waist I was conscious of. That scanty garment enhanced the softness of her sensitive thighs, the fragile bodice only half-captured her breasts, showed white shoulders and her naked back. I was breathing heavily, suddenly very hot.

"I'm sorry about this," I said thickly.

Her blue eyes were looking up into mine, and she wasn't worrying about the chain any more, wasn't thinking about it. She was trembling the same as me, and half rose towards me when I realized what she wanted and bent over her, took her in my arms.

Her body was quivery and excited. Her lips warmly moist and exploring. Her fingers were hot and urgent as they encircled my neck, pulled me down with her.

There must have been quite a blaze raging, without either of us realizing it. It flared up suddenly, consumed us in a hot, breathless moment of time. So fierce was the embrace, her lips bruised mine. When she broke away with a sharp, shuddering intake of breath, I felt blood on my lips.

She was breathing unbelievably fast. Her hot fingers on my neck were guiding my head. "Lee," she gasped, almost inaudibly. "Lee!"

"Honey," I panted. "I never ..."

Her fingers were round my neck and were burning. "Lee," she panted. "Kiss me. Kiss me the way you did that first time."

She hadn't forgotten it. I hadn't forgotten it either. The memory of it had haunted me so I'd had to ruthlessly dismiss it from my mind to get to sleep at nights.

"Aw, honey," I breathed. I kissed her. Her fingers went around my neck and were steely bands of anticipation, as detaining as the chain around her waist. She gave a long, drawn-out sigh of pleasure. There was that hot haze at the back of my brain again. She drew another deep breath like she was gonna sigh, but instead said:

"This chain, Lee. It's hurting me."

It was a delicate, sensitive moment. She exploded it with that attempt to exploit my emotions. I pressed my head back against her detaining fingers, stared into her eyes and said, levelly: "You're not getting loose until I'm good and ready."

Her eyes were dreamily happy but hurt. "But I promise you, Lee. I won't make any attempt to get away. I promise you that."

"That chain's a whole lot safer than any promises," I said grimly.

The hurt filled her eyes. Then, with the sudden strength of anger, she pushed me away from her, brought her knees up so she could push me away forcibly.

"Get away from me," she snarled. "Why can't you keep away from me?"

I got up slowly, straightened my collar. She'd curled up on the bed away from me, glaring angrily as she pulled her shoulder-strap back on her arm.

"Quite the Mata Hari, aren't you?" I sneered.

"You're a fool," she snapped. "You're a great fool!"

Jessica murmured loudly in her drugged sleep. She moved herself around, levered herself into a different position. What she was doing made me blush and avert my eyes from Helen. I went out to the bathroom, came back with a small pot of ointment. I tossed it to Helen. She caught it automatically. "What's this for?" she asked.

"For the place where the chain's been rubbing."

It was a glass pot, and I dodged just in time. It smashed to pieces against the wall immediately in line with my head.

CHAPTER FOURTEEN

Frisk arrived five minutes before time. I stood in a doorway, watched him pull into the kerbside. I was concealed in the doorway. I wasn't taking any chances. I wanted to be convinced Frisk had come alone and had no bodyguards lurking at a discreet distance.

Frisk was nervous and anxious. At five past nine, he got out of the car, peered in both directions along the intersection. If he had been expecting to meet a man, he'd have stood a chance of noticing me. As it was, he was expecting to meet Jessica. His eyes were only for dames. That enabled me to sidle close to him, shelter myself in a doorway just a few yards from his car.

He gave up at last, shot one more furious glance up and down the intersection, hurled a cigarette on the sidewalk and ground it viciously under his heel. Then he stalked back to his car, climbed in with a to-hell-with-it-all manner. There weren't many folk around, but there were enough. It wasn't exactly the place to hijack a guy. But this looked like being my only chance of getting really close to Frisk when he wasn't with his bodyguard. I got the back door of his car open as he was reaching for the ignition key. I moved swiftly and smoothly, slamming the car door behind me and sliding along the seat until I was behind him. As he turned, his startled face stared into the muzzle of the automatic I'd bought that same afternoon in a junk shop.

"Take it easy, Frisk," I said softly. "I can't miss at this range."

That guy sure was yella. He went grey. His lips quivered and his face began to work. I was scared he'd spoil everything by just sheer funk, be goaded by fear into making a desperate break that no courageous man would have risked.

"Face around front," I growled grimly. "Not one peep out of you, Frisk. Not one movement without I tell you. You framed me for killing Manton. If I've gotta die for him, I'll die for you too."

He faced around front, hands on the steering-wheel.

His hands were trembling like he had the ague. I was right behind him. Just to remind him, I pressed the cold tip of the gun on the back of his neck. His hair prickled and his skin crawled.

"Get yourself under control," I instructed. "And start driving."

For the first hundred yards, he drove like a learner. Then, as he was compelled to concentrate on his driving, it helped to steady his nerves. He obeyed my instructions implicitly, crossed the city towards the highroad that led to my house. From time to time, I glanced behind. It didn't look like I was being followed. When we reached the outskirts of town and the street lights began to drop behind us, leaving only the open road and darkness, he managed to get better control of himself.

"I can get you out of this," he promised hoarsely. "I've got dough, plenty of dough. You don't have to kill me. You can have all the dough you want. You can take a powder. I'll pay off the cops so they forget about it."

"You could have done that before."

"I was crazy," he pleaded. "I didn't know what I was doing. I was scared what might happen to me."

"I'm still scared," I said grimly.

Three or four miles outta town, I made him pull off the main road onto the grass verge where I'd parked my own car. When he pulled up, he was trembling all over. I could tell he thought this was where he was going to get it. I cut across his new burst of pleading.

"Cut it out, Frisk," I rasped. "I ain't going to kill you. You're going to be my insurance against being hung."

"I don't want to die," he choked. "I'll do anything you want – anything!"

"Just lean forward and put your hands behind your back," I instructed. "That's all I want for the moment."

I'd brought lengths of thin wire with me. I secured his wrists behind his back, content in the knowledge he couldn't even struggle without cutting himself badly. Another length of thin wire I formed into a noose, slipped it quickly over his head and drew it tight enough to be painful. He became rigid all over, like he thought just breathing might cause that wire to bite deeply and kill.

"Don't get scared," I growled. "There's more to it than just killing you. You ain't gonna die for a long while ... yet!"

We changed over, got into my car. He came reluctantly but obediently. I drove with one hand, the length of thin wire in my other. He was completely at my mercy. If he made just one wrong move, I had only to tug on that wire. A real hard pull would sever his jugular vein in the same way wire cuts through cheese.

When we reached my house, he was so scared that his legs were rubbery. He stumbled up the steps. I opened up, took him up the stairs to my room. There was a long moment of pregnant silence while Helen stared at him wide-eyed. He stared back at her. His white tongue tried to moisten his colourless lips. "Don't let him kill me," he pleaded desperately. "Don't let him kill me."

"I told you," I growled. "You ain't gonna die ... yet! But you can start in talking. Tell this dame how you killed Manton. Tell her how you tried to frame it on me."

He was a pathetic figure, all the confidence and bounce gone out of him. He was ready to sink to his knees. But fear of death, from whichever direction it might come, was strong within him. He looked at me furtively, looked at the girl. "It's a trap," he said. "He's trying to force me to make a confession. I didn't kill Manton. He killed him."

Overwhelming anger and fury consumed me. For one blind second, I was fighting the temptation to throw my full weight back so that the thin wire became a razor, shearing halfway through his neck. When the red rage subsided and I realized that I had won the battle, I was sweating, trembling.

Helen said: "It's true what he says. You can't extort a confession from him. It doesn't mean a thing in a court of law."

I brushed the back of my hand across my forehead. "I wanted you to know," I said. "I wanted you to understand the way it was."

"I believe you, Lee," she said simply.

Frisk said, desperately: "He's trying to frame me. He killed Manton. He's trying to save himself."

There was dull hopelessness inside me. If Frisk wasn't prepared to admit to the cops he'd killed Manton in self-defence as I'd suggested, he certainly wouldn't be willing to admit it now.

I said, wearily: "Okay, Frisk, let's go."

His face went green. "No," he jibbered. "You can't kill me. You can't kill me. It's murder."

I tugged gently on the wire. "You ain't gonna die," I told him again. "Not unless you won't do what I say."

He followed me downstairs. He had to. He was gibbering and moaning with terror the whole time. It was worse when I opened the door to the cellars, leading him down steep wooden stairs. But there wasn't a thing he could do about it, not with that razor-keen circle around his neck.

I took him to the far corner of the cellar, forced him down on his knees. He was sweating blood then, sobbing for mercy and almost grovelling. I'd fastened heavy iron shackles to his waist and ankles before he realized what was happening. I attached more heavy chains to his wrists, before releasing them from the wire. And then the final humiliation. I firmly secured another heavy chain around his neck. Only then did I loose him of the wire noose.

He didn't understand it. "What are you doing?" he quavered. "What are you going to do to me?"

I walked over to the door. He clambered to his feet, staggered across to me. He was bowed down by the weight of the chains. Every step he took caused a loud clanking. His voice was frantic. "You can't do this to me. It's inhuman. You've gotta let me go or I'll go crazy."

I stood in the doorway, let him see the bitter smile that curled around my lips. The chains brought him up short just before he reached the doorway. He'd be just able to reach the food slid in to him.

"You've gotta let me go," he wailed. "You can't do this to me. You must be crazy."

"It'll give you something to think about, Frisk," I said grimly. "This is gonna be your new home. You're gonna live here day and night, chained down the way you are now, alone and without light of any kind. You'll have food once a day, slid in to you through a gap at the bottom of the door." I paused meaningfully. "Some time tonight there isn't going to be any more door. Because I'm going to get busy with bricks and cement, sealing up this cellar, so it becomes your tomb."

His eyes were wild, bulging from their sockets.

I went on, brutally and viciously. "You'll lie here in the darkness, alone and unaided, weighed down by those chains, your body becoming a mass of festering sores where the chains rub your flesh. You'll lie here for hour after hour, thinking of all the things you've done, remembering every little incident in your life. You'll lie here, mouldering and rotting in the darkness, your body cramped and dying, and all the time thinking of freedom, delicious, wonderful freedom. The desire for it will grow ever bigger in your mind, and your brain will expand and expand, constantly seeking for freedom. And then, one day ..." I paused and moistened my lips ... "One day, your brain will expand to its utter most. With sudden lighting clarity it will burst. And then you will be free. Free from your confinement in this cellar, free from the chains and free from the mental agony. You'll be free from this world, Frisk. You'll be free because you will become ... insane!"

The vehemence and brutality of my words stunned him. He sagged to his knees, stared at me with bulging eyes and incomprehension. It was too much for him to take in. He couldn't believe this was really happening to him.

"I'll be back a little later," I said grimly. "I'll be back to wall you in, brick by brick, until you are sealed off from the rest of the world. Sealed off so the rest of the world will not hear your maniacal moanings and jibberings." I paused again, breathed deeply. "And while I'm gone, you can think back over the past, remember all the things you've done that you shouldn't. Maybe you'll remember that my name is Lee. That I'm your stepson. And then, you'll really understand what's happening."

I switched off the light abruptly, plunged him into darkess. As I went up the stairs, I heard him begin to shriek. That suited me fine. The more he shrieked, the sooner he'd crack. I wanted to see him crazy. I wanted to see him stark raving mad, frothing at the mouth, throwing himself around like a wild animal.

As I closed the door at the top of the stairs, it cut off the screams abruptly. That was because I'd lined the door with felt with this particular motive in mind.

When I got upstairs, Helen's blue eyes were watching me with an enigmatic expression the moment I entered the door. I'd been too preoccupied with Frisk to notice it before. I noticed it now.

"Where's Jessica?" I demanded. "What's happened to her?"

"She skipped," said Helen. "She brightened up not long after you left, started looking around."

"I don't believe it," I said. "She wouldn't go. Not without ..."

"She found the capsules," said Helen. "She looked through the drawers, found them in that cabinet."

"That finishes it," I sighed. "I wanted to fix her so she didn't talk."

She said quietly: "You've got me on a chain. I guess by now you've got Frisk on a chain. Did you want to have her on a chain, too? What are you going to do? Chain the whole world?"

"Listen, Helen," I said quietly. "I told you Frisk was my main concern. Well, I've got him now. I'm gonna release you tomorrow. I've got it all worked out. You were unconscious when I brought you here. You don't know where in hell you are. Tonight I'm gonna blindfold you, take you in your car to a place many miles from here. I'm gonna dump the car where it will be found in the morning, leave you tied up in the car. I'm gonna take your word for it that you won't squawk to the cops."

Her eyes were tender but strangely pained. "Why did you wait till now?" she pleaded. "You could have trusted me at the beginning. I promised I wouldn't hurt you in any way."

"I've got Frisk now," I said grimly.

"What about Manton's daughter?" she asked. "She knows where this house is. She might cause trouble."

"I'll leave here myself tomorrow," I said. "She can tell the cops. They'll come and find the place, search it and find it empty."

"And what about Frisk?"

"I'll leave him enough grub for a week. I'm gonna brick him in tonight. It's unlikely the cops will carry out a search. The dame's got nothing to gain by going to the cops."

"Listen, Lee," she said softly. "I'm glad you're gonna let me go tonight. And there's one more thing I'm going to say. Whatever happens. I mean ... if at any time ..."

It was a loud, thunderous knock at the door. It cut through her words, caused her to glance at me sharply and caused my heart to beat more rapidly.

"Perhaps it's Jessica come back," she said.

"Maybe," I said. "Maybe not. Let them take it out on the knocker."

The hammering at the door continued. I crept down the stairs, peeped out through the window by the side of the door. It was dark, but I could see the outline of a short, tubby little guy. He was raising the knocker again to start a new fusilade as I opened the door.

"Ah, good evening," he said.

I stared at him. "What d'you want?" I growled.

"I saw a light," he said. "I knew there was somebody here."

The light upstairs was at the back of the house. I said, suspiciously: "You been nosing around?"

"It's like this, fella," he said. "Just got a little car trouble. Right down the bottom here, outside your gate. Haven't got a jack with me. Would you be a good guy and lend me a jack?"

"Haven't got a jack," I growled. "Try some other place." I started to close the door.

"That's tough," he said. Then he added quickly: "Just a minute, mister. Don't shut the door. What about that other car halfway down the drive? Has he got a jack?"

"What other car?" I asked.

"There's a car parked halfway up your drive," he said. "Must be friends of yours. Would they have a jack?"

My spine began to crawl. I wondered whether Frisk's bodyguards had been following after all, perhaps even now were waiting for Frisk to reappear.

"I only want it for a moment," he said. "Just to jack up the back wheel. So if it's okay with your friends ..."

I came out through the door, stood at the top of the steps and peered down the drive. I couldn't see any car. I turned to the fat little guy as his arms encircled mine, clasped them in a steely grip that didn't go with his voice. At the same moment, other figures swooped out of the shadows, rough hands grasping me, torchlights shining in my face. I caught glimpse of uniforms, heard hard, authoritative voices issuing orders, and realized the strong hands grasping me were too many to resist. It was the cops. They seemed to know exactly what they were doing. Jessica was a great help. She led the way to the first floor, acting like this was the greatest moment of her life.

They crowded me into my room, the cop chief gave one look at Helen, issued swift instructions. Before I realized what was happening, steel bracelets encircled my wrists.

The cop chief said, grimly: "Get her loose."

One of the cops gouged his knuckles into the back of my neck. "Where's the key, lady-snatcher?"

I gulped. Everything had happened so quickly I could hardly believe it was turning out this way. "My trouser pocket," I said like I was in a dream.

They got the key, three of them supporting Helen, while another loosened the chain around her waist. She didn't need any supporting but, dressed the way she was, the cops were willing to give her plenty of service. And all the time, her blue eyes were staring into mine, anxious and pained.

The cop who'd released the chain, stood up abruptly and strode over towards me. I saw the anger in his black, hate-filled eyes a fraction of a second before his knuckles smashed my lips. I'd have hit the floor if there hadn't been all those other cops holding me up. "You damned swine," he roared. "Treating a dame like that!" He drew back his arm to slam his knuckles in my face again.

Helen shrieked a protest at the same time as the cops chief's hard, clear voice rapped at him: "Cut that out, Walters. He'll get all that's coming to him."

I was dazed now. My lips were swelling rapidly. There were so many cops holding me, I felt their rough hands were bruising me all over. There was another group of cops surrounding Helen, offering her consolation, pulling sheets off the bed to drape around her, sympathising with her while they said harsh things about me. She too was acting like she was in a dream, ignoring them and staring deep into my eyes.

It needed Jessica to draw the complete picture. She pushed through the cops to Helen. "I did it, honey," she said. "I did what you told me." She paused, took a deep breath and added eagerly: "When do I get the twenty-five thousand dollars reward?"

Across an abyss of time and space, Helen's blue eyes were looking into mine. She knew that I knew. It had been she who had told Jessica where she could find her precious dope. She'd promised Jessica a reward of twenty-five thousand dollars to bring the cops back with her.

I didn't care about anything any longer. It was all so hopeless. I'd tried and I'd failed. And now everything was a bigger mess than ever.

"Come on," rasped the cop chief. "Let's go. Let's get this guy in the can."

"Just a minute, Captain," said Helen. Her voice was low but commanding. He turned and looked at her respectfully. Any dame with a millionaire father is entitled to respect. Her blue eyes were watching me, were still strangely tender and pained when she said, quietly:

"You'd better go down to the basement. Captain. You'll find another man chained up there. He was going to brick him in tonight."

CHAPTER FIFTEEN

It was knowing Helen was responsible that hurt most. For years I'd planned my revenge on Frisk. Then my moment of triumph had been snatched from me by Helen.

I couldn't blame her. She'd had a tough time, chained up that way. I couldn't blame her wanting to get loose. But the irony of it was she should have turned the tables on me as I was getting ready to release her.

Yeah, it was Helen that hurt most. Sitting in the cell with all that time on my hands enabled me to realize lots of things. I was realizing Frisk wasn't so important after all. It was Helen dominating my thoughts. I couldn't stop thinking about her, the way she looked curled up on the bed in her scanty underclothing, the blueness of her eyes, the intonation of her voice and the softness of her skin.

What was worse was knowing I wasn't likely to see her again, except in court. What happened after the trial, I didn't want to think about. I had a kinda numbed feeling in my belly. Maybe it was as well. It stopped me feeling the futility of everything.

I'd called in a mouthpiece. He wasn't good, but he was the best I could afford with what was left of my savings. He came along to my cell, smartly dressed and with a brand new leather briefcase. He acted like he owned the jail, sent the warder away after he was locked in with me, sat on the bunk opposite me, settled himself comfortably and stared at me solemnly. He shook his head slowly. "Boy, what a jam you're in!"

"Look, Mr Shepherd," I said. "I haven't asked you ..."

"Jordan's the name," he said. "I'm your solicitor. Jordan."

"What about Shepherd?"

"He's passed the case over to me," he said with satisfaction.

His attitude irritated me. "What the hell?" I said. "I asked for Shepherd. I'm paying Shepherd. I didn't ask you."

"Look," he said slowly. "Whoever you ask in this town, he's gonna send me in. Get that understood."

"You telling me I can't have what solicitor I choose?"

He opened the briefcase, brushed away my question with a careless wave of his hand. "Let's get down to facts," he said. "Get back to realities. Now, I suppose you know what you're up against?"

I swallowed, opened my mouth to argue. Then relaxed again. What was the good of it? It would all come to the same in the end.

"I don't know the charges," I said. "I didn't listen."

"They're pretty considerable," he said. He almost smacked his lips. "First, there's the charge of killing Manton. It's a tough one. Helen Gaskin was a witness to seeing you in the car with the murdered man. The cops have got your fingerprints now. They match up very nicely with a set of fingerprints found on an empty whisky bottle and the fingerprints on the steering wheel.

"It was a frame-up," I said hollowly.

"No doubt," he said cheerfully. He consulted a sheaf of papers. "What next? Ah, yes. You kidnapped Miss Gaskin. There doesn't seem to be the slightest doubt about that. She was found in premises rented by you. Then there's the question of Frisk. You kidnapped him too. An influential businessman."

"He framed me," I said hollowly.

He grinned. "The prosecution wouldn't agree. They'd say you tried to frame Frisk. They'd say you imprisoned him, tried to extort a confession from him for a crime he didn't commit."

"Just the same, he framed me," I said doggedly.

"Looks like you're in real trouble," he said happily. "Charged with murdering Manton. Charged with the kidnapping of Miss Gaskin. Charged with kidnapping Mr Manton. All capital offences, and all exacting the penalty of death if proved."

I glared at him. "Are you supposed to be my solicitor, or are you practising for a song and dance on my coffin?"

"We'll see, we'll see," he said. He put his hands in his pockets, looked up at the ceiling. "Let's get one thing quite clear before we go any further. Whatever you say, you're my client and I'm defending you. So I must have full facts. Understand? Full facts. If you're guilty or not, it's just the same to me. I'm just out to get you off."

"You haven't a hope."

"That's the kinda talk," he said, "that I like to hear. Now answer me this question: are you guilty of these charges or not?"

"I'm not," I said.

He took a pad from his briefcase, a pencil from his pocket and looked at me with grey eyes that seemed to penetrate my brain. "Now, just what were you doing the night Manton was killed?" he asked.

I hadn't liked him at first. But his questions were so shrewd and so embracing, I grudgingly grew to respect his abilities. He was there for maybe three hours, stabbing questions at me, checking and counter-checking. Not once did he trip me up. There was a good reason for that. I had nothing to hide. I told him everything, just the way it was.

Finally he heaved a sigh, climbed to his feet and said with satisfaction: "I guess that's just about all I wanna know. Of course, it's a hopeless case. But maybe we'll dig out one or two things that will cheer you up." He grinned encouragingly. "I'm sending to New York for Bailey to act as your counsel."

I stared at him. "J T Bailey?" I asked.

He nodded, grinned expansively. "That's the guy. You've heard of him, of course."

"But that's crazy," I protested. "A guy like him costs dough. I've barely got enough to cover your expenses."

He winked. "Bailey's a friend of mine," he said. "He'll come." He shrugged his shoulders. "It'll be publicity for him."

* * *

It was four weeks before I came up for trial. Throughout that time, I hadn't seen anybody. Since that first interview, I'd not seen Jordan either. I'd had four weeks of lonely confinement, four weeks to sit and meditate by myself. Four weeks to realize that Frisk was sitting pretty and the chances of my getting even a life sentence were very slim.

You can die a thousand times in four weeks that way. I died a thousand times. But every time I died, the bitterness of it was made more poignant by the knowledge I wouldn't be seeing Helen again.

Yeah, that was the rub. In the brief days that Helen had been my captive, something had happened to me. That dame had got deep down inside me. There was something about her that got me.

Yeah, that was the hell of it. I wouldn't ever see her again. It had been a short, sweet episode. Something to remember. A queer thought, that. Something to remember when, at the last moment, I was waiting for the warder to throw that switch.

* * *

The courtroom was crowded and stuffy. There seemed half-a-million folk there, and every one of them was trying to look at me. I sat with folded arms, looking neither to left nor right and vaguely understanding this was a battle for my life in which I had no part. My solicitor Jordan was there, the first time I'd seen him since that preliminary interview.

The tall, hawk-nosed guy quizzing the jury members was Bailey, who'd come down from New York especially to defend my case.

Nobody does anything for nothing. I guessed he wanted the publicity of it all. Well, if it was publicity he wanted, he was certainly gonna get it. Because not many guys appear in the dock with three separate charges against them, each of which merits the death sentence.

The testing and selection of the jury members went on for hours. The court adjourned for lunch, and I was locked away downstairs, supplied with milk and sandwiches. Then it was back to the court again. It was two days before the jury were finally selected and sworn in. The third day, the prosecuting counsel opened his case.

Listening to him, I knew everything was hopeless. First of all, there were the witnesses who had found Manton's body in the car, the doctors, the ballistics experts and the fingerprints experts. They tied me in with Manton properly. My fingerprints were found all over the car. Just to make it neat and tidy was the evidence supplied by Helen.

The prospect of seeing her in court was the one thing that had given me any interest in the trial. I wanted one more look at her, have her blue eyes looking deep into mine.

But she was too ill to attend court. The prosecuting counsel waved her statement, which she'd made on oath, added gently that she'd undergone a gruelling experience that had caused her nervous shock. He added, meaningfully, that later, the jury members would understand the ordeal she had undergone. Then, very slowly and very loudly, he read her statement. It was brief and to the point. It made it quite clear how she'd seen me in the car with Manton.

It kinda hurt, knowing she was giving the evidence that would provide Frisk with his final victory. Yet all she did was to tell the truth. Her statement was made on oath. What other information could she give?

It took two days for the prosecuting counsel to complete his case. Hour by hour, the evidence piled up, one strong brick added carefully to another strong brick, building a wall that was stronger and more confining in every way than the one with which I had intended to seal Frisk off from all mankind. I could sense now the hostility of the public. As the facts slowly emerged, the reporters were phoning them through to the newspapers. Public feeling was running high against me. I was a cold-blooded murderer. What was more, I was a bestial kidnapper. Nothing could stop those newshounds. I was in court charged only with murdering Manton. The kidnapping charge would follow later, if I was able to get free from the murder charge. But the newspapers weren't missing a thing. The kidnapping took the public interest. It was built up really big.

With so much public feeling against me, a public hatred that was harsh and implacable, it irritated me to see the way Jordan the solicitor sat easily and comfortably throughout the hearing, a gentle smile whispering around his lips. And as for Bailey, whatever great guns he may have been in New York, he wasn't firing many shots now. He spent little time in the court, leaving his junior to conduct the case.

I didn't know why they were taking so long about it. I didn't understand why they had to go through all this rigmarole. I was innocent, but I had as much chance as a celluloid cat in hell of proving it. The evidence was so thick against me, no sane jury member could find me innocent.

But that was up until the time the prosecution rested its case. Then, abruptly, the whole nature of the trial changed. Bailey, the defending counsel, came back into court with the air of a gladiator about to meet the lions. His eyes gleamed and his hawk-nose seemed eager to rend and tear his prey. He threw overboard every conventional court procedure and refrained from addressing the jury, beyond telling them the evidence he was about to draw out in court could completely contradict the charges of the prosecutor.

He called his first witness. "Miss Susan Long."

I'd never heard the name before. I craned my neck with the others, wanting to see who she was. It wasn't until she was seated in the witness box and pulled back the wispy little veil to her hat that I recognised the bony dame who'd been losing so heavily that night at Frisk's nightclub.

Bailey was gentle with her, drawing her out smoothly and easily. His voice was that of a loving father extracting from his daughter a full account of her evening's outing.

"And what did you do in the backroom of this nightclub?" he asked.

Susan took a deep breath. "I was playing a game," she said. "Lots of people went back to play games."

A chuckle ran around the court. Everyone knew Frisk ran a gambling joint. Everyone knew the cops knew it. But the cops didn't like it talked about. They were satisfied with the cut they got, but didn't like criticism, didn't like it inferred they weren't doing their duty.

Bailey's hooked nose hovered over Susan like he was about to pounce on her. But his voice was oily, smooth. "While you were playing your ... game! ... did you notice particularly anyone else who was also playing?"

"There were a number of people I noticed," faltered Susan.

Bailey looked at the ceiling disinterestedly. "Will you look around the courtroom and see if you can identify any of those players?"

Susan looked around. Her eyes rested on me, lighted up and her bony chest heaved. Her long thin arm was fully extended.

"That man there," she said.

Bailey didn't even bother to look. "Did you notice him for any particular reason?"

"Why yes," she said eagerly. "He was right next to me, and he was, ..." She broke off suddenly remembering the cops. She amended her statement hurriedly. "He was playing the same game as me."

Another chuckle ran around the court. The judge frowned over his glasses, looked around. "This is not a music-hall," he said sternly.

I was the next witness on the stand. I hadn't seen my solicitor, I hadn't even thought I'd be called. I felt all those eyes watching me as I went to the witness box, took my seat.

Bailey said: "I want you to tell the court your story. Exactly the way you told it to Mr Jordan, your solicitor. Tell us everything that happened, in the greatest detail."

I licked my lips nervously. I stared at him anxiously. "Will it do any good?"

"Don't quibble," he snapped. "Just do what I tell you. Tell your whole story."

I swallowed, gulped, realized Bailey must have something up his sleeve, and plunged into my account of what had happened. I particularly mentioned Frisk's name. I particularly mentioned how he'd killed Manton.

There was a kinda stunned silence in court when I was through. The DA had some questions to ask me. He too looked a little shaken.

"Now tell me," he said pompously. "Are you of the opinion that if anyone had killed Manton and wished to put the blame on someone else, he could have invented a better story than the one you have sat there and alleged actually happened?"

"Objection," yelled Bailey.

"Objection sustained," said the judge.

But the DA had got over his point. It dealt a heavy blow at my story. He went on questioning. Subtle, artful questioning that, while it was unable to shake my story, provided reasonable doubt in the minds of the jurymen.

When at last the ordeal was over and I was allowed to creep back to my seat, the usher called loudly for the next witness. "Miss Diana Foster."

I knew who she was. The dame I'd danced with. She smiled around the court when she entered, crossed her legs carelessly as she sat on the stand, and as soon as she saw me, nodded warmly.

My solicitor musta been doing a lotta digging. It musta cost plenty of dough. The way these witnesses were turning up showed he'd exploited every little detail I'd given him, followed them through and was squeezing every possible advantage from them.

Bailey questioned her with care, every question making itself felt. "And after you had danced with Mr Shelton, what happened then?"

"Mr Shelton left," she said. "He went to the backroom of the nightclub."

"And then?"

She flushed. "I was lonely," she admitted. "My brother and his fiancee left early. I decided I'd join Mr Shelton in the games room. But when I got there, he wasn't to be seen."

"You concluded then Mr Shelton must have left and gone home?"

"Oh no," she said, scandalized. "That was impossible."

"Why?"

She flushed, shot me a shy, sideways glance. "Mr Shelton was very nice," she said. "I was awaiting an opportunity to see him again. I was watching the door all the time. He couldn't possibly have left the club."

"Then what conclusions did you form?"

"There was only one place he could have been," she said. "He must have been in Mr Frisk's office."

"But you couldn't prove that?" Bailey shot at her.

She shook her head. "No, I couldn't prove it. Not directly."

"Could you prove it indirectly?"

Once again she flushed. "I stayed until the nightclub closed. I knew Mr Shelton would be sure to come out. I went to the car park, got my car and drove back to the front of the nightclub. It was closed then, but there was a light inside. I decided to wait for half-an-hour. But before then, Mr Shelton came out."

"He came out alone?"

She shook her head. "No," she said ruefully. "He seemed to be under the weather. The two men with him were supporting him. He looked as though he'd had too much to drink. They helped him into a car, drove off with him."

"Can you describe the car?"

"Yes. A dark blue or a black saloon."

"Would you recognise those two men who were with Mr Shelton?"

"I recognised them immediately. I've seen them many times before."

Bailey turned to the judge.

Bailey said quickly: "Your Honour, may I request leave to recall this witness to the stand at a later date?"

"Objection," yelled the DA automatically.

The judge stared at him blankly. "Why?"

The DA hadn't thought of his reason yet. "Why ... because ..." His voice trailed off as his mind groped for a reason.

The judge banged his gavel on his desk. "Objection overruled."

The next witness was Gunn. He was dressed to kill, lounged contemptuously into the courtroom, sat elegantly in the witness box and sneered around as if to say: "*Well, this is so very childish.*"

The prosecution was getting worried. The case had taken an unusual turn. The DA's face was hard and intent when Bailey began his questioning.

"Look at the accused," he said. "Do you recognise him?"

"Sure," said Gunn, looking at me and flashing his teeth. "He's a hophead. Musta misjudged. Gave himself too big a jolt while he was in our club. Passed right out on the office floor."

I took a deep breath. I knew what was coming. Just for a little while, I'd dared to hope. Now again I could see it was no good trying to break this case against me. It was too strong.

"That was the night Manton was murdered?"

His smile slipped a little. "I guess it would be," Gunn conceded.

"What did you do with Shelton when he passed out on your office floor?" asked Bailey.

Gunn shrugged. "What else could we do? He was cluttering up the place. Me and Jenks took him in the car, left him on a park bench to cool off." His eyes glittered with malevolent amusement. "Maybe we shouldn't have left him. He was a hophead. Everyone knows hopheads get murderous. Maybe we shouldn't have left him alone. Maybe Manton wouldn't have been killed and ..."

"Confine yourself to answering questions," snapped Bailey.

"Yes, sir," said Gunn. His smile flashed at the jury. They listened intently, lapped up every word he let drop.

Bailey put on an act. He looped his thumbs in his vest armholes, looked at the ceiling and rocked back on his heels. Then he said, very gently: "Supposing it was suggested you and your associate Jenks drove to a disused parking lot nearby and left Mr Shelton in a car that had been stolen, returning again to the nightclub to collect the body of Manton, who had recently been shot by Mr Frisk. Would you call that a lie?"

"I sure would," said Gunn. He bristled with indignation. "Anyone who would say that is a damned liar. He'd have to suffer, too. There's a law in this country!"

"I sympathise with you," mocked Bailey. "And if it was further suggested the body of Manton was placed in the back of that stolen car and that you and Jenks then drove that stolen car onto the highroad, left it parked in such a way that when it was discovered, it might easily be assumed Shelton had murdered Manton, that, too, would be a lie?"

Gunn said hotly: "I've never heard such an outrageous suggestion."

Bailey grinned at him. There was something special about the way he grinned. Like he knew something that Gunn didn't. "You categorically deny Frisk shot Manton?" he asked.

"We hadn't seen Manton there for two weeks prior to his death."

Bailey looked at his fingernails. He said, softly: "Murder is a very serious crime. Men are executed for it."

Gunn licked his lips. "Why tell me?"

Bailey turned to the judge. "Your Honour," he said, "may I recall my previous witness for a moment, without this gentleman leaving the stand?"

The judge opened his mouth to speak, but already Bailey had beckoned to Diane Foster. She stood up, walked over to him.

"In the previous evidence you referred to two men," he said. "Can you identify any of them in this court?"

"I sure can," said Diane. She pointed an accusing finger at Gunn. "This is one of them."

Bailey beamed with satisfaction. "That's all," he said. "Kindly sit down again."

There was a rustle of expectancy among the onlookers as she returned to her seat. And whereas before, Bailey had been almost gentle with Gunn, now he changed, turned into a terrifying symbol of justice. He stood well back from Gunn, asked in thunderous, terrifying tones. "Will you tell the court how long you have been outside, waiting to be called to the stand?"

Gunn was nervous. "I guess maybe an hour-and-a-half."

"And throughout that time, you have had no manner or means of learning the nature of the evidence given by these witnesses who appeared before you?"

Gunn was wary. His brow puckered. "I guess not," he said hesitantly.

"You have just heard this woman identify you!"

Gunn had lost his grin. "Yeah, that's right ... I don't know ..."

"Do you know the penalty for murder?"

"Look here ... What is ...?"

"Do you know the penalty for murder?" thundered Bailey. "Answer yes or no."

"Yes," said Gunn reluctantly.

"Are you aware three or four or a dozen men equally guilty by complicity in the murder of just one man can all be charged and executed?"

Gunn's face was white. "What are you getting at?"

Bailey had got him scared. His advantage was Gunn didn't know what evidence had already been given. He was getting Gunn shaken, making it clear to him that if any charge was brought against Gunn, Frisk and Jenks, they might all be faced with a murder charge. He wanted to make Gunn realize that covering up for Frisk under such circumstances might be a risk to his own neck.

Bailey was playing his trump card now. He leaned forward, black eyes glittering and hook-nose looming revengefully. "I want you to think carefully before you answer my next question. I want you to understand that if and when my client is declared innocent of the charge laid against him, that of murdering Manton, it may transpire the prosecution will make other charges."

The flamboyance had seeped out of Gunn. His knuckles showed white where he gripped the sides of the chair. Bailey deliberately allowed seconds to pass before he continued, long seconds throughout which the silence of the courtroom was deafening.

"You are speaking here on oath. Any statements you make are being recorded. Such statements can be used again in open court. Your truthfulness can be judged in the light of other evidence that is produced." He paused again.

Gunn was sweating now. His face was white, and the sweat stood out on his brow like he was in a Turkish bath. "It may easily transpire," said Bailey, "that a man accused of murder may implicate associates deliberately in order to distract attention from his own guilt. There have been many such cases, some of which have been tried in this very courtroom."

Gunn was staring at him as though hypnotised.

"It is not my duty to give you this warning," said Bailey. "But I am aware of the seriousness of your situation. I cannot permit myself to ask you to answer this final question without giving you due warning."

Bailey certainly earned his dough. He'd almost convinced me the previous witnesses had given full testimony completely incriminating Frisk.

"Think well before you answer this last question," intoned Bailey solemnly. He held the court now. "Who killed Manton?"

Gunn looked around desperately as though seeking assistance. The DA was trying to catch his eye, shake his head to warn him it was a trick. But Bailey moved easily, kept himself between Gunn and the DA. "Answer up," he rapped sharply. "You don't have to think about this. You've had all the time you need for thinking. This is the time for answers. Do you know who murdered Manton?"

Gunn bit his lip. A hunted look came into his eyes. The sweat was running down his cheeks now. He was fighting an internal struggle with himself like he was trying to make a denial but the words wouldn't come out.

"You must answer the question," said the judge.

Gunn jerked his head sideways to stare at him. His lips moved but his tongue seemed too big. He made another effort. The words kinda tore themselves from his mouth. "It was self-defence," he burst out.

A kinda gasp ran around the courtroom. Bailey followed up his advantage immediately.

"Be more explicit. You say it was self-defence. But who was trying to defend himself? Who shot Manton? Who put those two bullets in his chest?"

Gunn's face was haggard. "I had nothing to do with it," he quavered. "Self-defence. Me and Jenks were only trying to help."

Bailey boomed forcibly: "Who killed Manton?"

Gunn hung his head. "It was Frisk," he said. "He shot him. It was Frisk."

CHAPTER SIXTEEN

The DA asked that the charges against me should be dropped, and immediately instituted proceedings against Frisk for the murder of Manton.

But I wasn't released. I was escorted to a cell beneath the courtroom and was there for maybe an hour before Jordan, my solicitor, smiling cheerfully and rubbing his hands with satisfaction, paid me a visit.

"I guess that takes care of Frisk," he said with satisfaction.

He was flushed with triumph. I wasn't. I'd known all along I was innocent. The verdict in my favour didn't make me feel triumphant, only mean and bitter.

"How soon do I get out of here?"

He eyed me cunningly. "You have to appear against Frisk as a witness, of course. Then there's the question of you kidnapping Frisk, imprisoning him. For a certainty, the DA won't prefer charges against you on that score."

"How soon do I get put of here?"

He looked at the ceiling, looked at his fingernails, pursed his lips. "There's still the charge of kidnapping Helen Gaskin."

"I didn't kidnap her," I said. "I had no choice but to keep her quiet while I cleared myself."

"It was kidnapping," he said ominously.

I sighed and my shoulders drooped. "They're gonna press that charge?"

He nodded slowly. "They probably will."

"How long ...?"

He shrugrged. "If the case goes against you, maybe twenty years." He smiled encouragingly. "But then, the case may not be pressed."

I glanced up at him quickly. I had the uneasy feeling he was playing with me.

"You can get out on bail," he said.

"Bail," I said eagerly. Then my heart sank. "How much?"

"Twenty-five grand."

"Jeepers," I groaned.

"I'll fix it," he said.

I stared at him. "What are you talking about?" I demanded. "I ain't got no twenty-five grand."

"I can arrange something."

I got to my feet. "Listen, Mr Jordan," I said grimly. "What makes? You've had private dicks digging away for weeks getting evidence that got me off a murder rap. You've employed a New York attorney whose fees are fabulous. I've given you all the dough I had, not quite a thousand dollars. Now you're telling me you're gonna put up bail of twenty-five grand. What's your angle? I don't see how you make a nickel out of it."

He smiled engagingly and evasively, called for the warder to let him out of the cell, and his last words were: "Don't worry about the bail, I'll fix it."

He did, too. Half-an-hour later, they came for me, took me upstairs to the office and made me sign a bond certificate.

I stared at them incredulously. "You mean I can go now?"

The desk sergeant nodded. "Yeah. We'll send for you when we want you."

I went out in a kinda daze, caught a taxi and automatically gave him the address of my house.

Three hours ago I'd been in court, listening to the evidence piling up against me. Now a miracle had happened. I was as good as cleared on two charges and out on bail for the charge of kidnapping Helen Gaskin.

It looked like I wasn't gonna get my revenge on Frisk. But it also looked as though Frisk was gonna get his comeuppance anyway. I'd be the principal witness against him. I'd assert the killing of Manton was sheer, cold-blooded murder. The way Frisk tried to frame me as the killer would also rate against him. I was getting my revenge legally, my own evidence and actions sending Frisk to the chair, or, if he was lucky, to a long term of imprisonment. If he survived, he would venture out into the world fifteen or twenty years from now, white-haired, shoulders bowed and with a negligible future. I paid off the driver at the foot of the drive, walked up to the grim and empty house. Seeing it again made me think of Helen, made me remember her blue eyes and her glistening hair. A fleeting mental picture of soft white thighs flecked with black lace underwear tortured me.

There was a kinda dull heaviness inside me as I climbed the stairs. I wouldn't be seeing Helen again. It was strange how you could go a whole lifetime and never think about anyone very much. Then, after only five days, not to be able to stop thinking about them.

I opened the door of my room, pushed inside.

She was there, sitting on the bed just the way I'd remembered seeing her during those last, sleepless nights when I'd been waiting for trial.

I gaped at her. Her blue eyes smiled back. She said, softly: "I was waiting for you, Lee."

I gulped, stared at her like she was a vision. She was, too. A vision of beauty, no longer scruffy and dishevelled, but carefully turned out, hair well brushed and rippling like spun-gold, a flame-red, beautifully tailored dress, sheer silk stockings and high-heeled shoes.

"Helen!" I gasped.

"Congratulations, Lee," she said gently. "I knew you'd win through. You had to be able to win through if you were telling the truth."

I still couldn't believe she was really there. But at the same time, my mind was working quickly, piecing fragments of ideas together. How had she known I was going to be released? I hadn't known myself! Why should my solicitor have employed the most expensive and famous attorney in New York?

"Helen," I said, with a note of understanding in my voice. "You did that. You've been paying my legal expenses."

"You're not angry, are you, Lee?" Her blue eyes were soft and expectant, her voice low and inviting.

"You shouldn't have done it."

She pouted. "But it was my fault you were in that jam. I had to help you. I had to do what I could."

"It wasn't your fault," I said. "You had a right to get away if you could. I was holding you against your will."

She looked at me strangely. "They won't press the kidnapping charge," she said. "That'll be dropped."

"I'm out on bail," I said. "Twenty-five grand bail." I narrowed my eyes. "I suppose you put up the bail, too?"

She nodded, eyes smiling. "But they'll drop that, Lee," she said. "They'll drop the charge of kidnapping. If they won't drop it of their own accord, we'll make them drop it."

I stared at her. "Maybe you won't press the charges, but the cops will."

"Not necessarily, Lee," she said gently. "Not if I wasn't ... kidnapped!"

I stared at her, trying to understand her meaning. She smiled back, artfully. Then she moved subtlely, so that for the first time I could see the silver glint around her waist, realized she'd chained herself the way I'd chained her.

"You won't need a chain to keep me here, Lee. But I'll wear it if you want."

I crossed to her quickly, examined the chain. "Where's the key?" I demanded.

She shrugged. "Does it matter?"

My head was in a whirl. Standing close to her, I could smell her perfume, see the softness of her skin, see the deep meaning in her eyes and remember the soft touch of her when I kissed her. "Listen, Helen," I panted. "I don't know what all this is about and ..."

"Don't you?" she interrupted. Her blue eyes were staring into mine with an intensity of feeling, as though she was willing me to do something. I had a pretty good idea what it was. I wanted to do it. I moistened my dry lips with my tongue. "Listen, Helen," I said. "You don't mean that ..."

"If it's what you want, Lee," she said quietly. "The cops can't imprison a man for kidnapping his own wife, can they?"

The beating of my heart was so loud it was deafening me. It was all too good to be true. I couldn't begin to believe this was happening.

When I didn't answer immediately, her blue eyes clouded over, her soft voice sounded choked. "That is ... if you want me, Lee."

If I wanted her!

I'd never wanted anything more. I didn't talk. I didn't have to. I moved in on her quickly, and there was fusion of dream and reality, the uniting of memories with reality. Her fingers were gripping my neck and the whiteness of her skin merged from the flame-red of her dress.

It was all over now. Frisk and revenge, the brutal planning and the grim ruthlessness. It was all over.

But there was a new beginning, too. Beginning right now. Without bitterness and remorse, but with happiness and new life.

Her fingers had unexpected strength and frantic eagerness as she pulled my head towards her. "Kiss me, Lee," she panted. "Kiss me."

HANK JANSON TITLES AVAILABLE FROM TELOS PUBLISHING

The Trials Of Hank Janson

Steve Holland

In January 1954 twelve jurors sat at the Old Bailey to hear charges of obscenity against seven crime novels written by the immensely popular Hank Janson, whose sexy thrillers had sold five million copies in only six years. Hank's publisher and distributor were found guilty and imprisoned and an arrest warrant put out for author.

The Trials of Hank Janson presents a full biography of that author – in reality, a man named Stephen D Frances – from his early life, through the highs and lows he experienced with the Janson novels, to his eventual decline and death in Spain, cut off from the character he had created.

In addition, respected researcher and pulp fiction historian Steve Holland gives, for the first time, a comprehensive account of the early 1950s Home Office crackdown on so-called 'obscene' paperbacks – of which the Janson novels were the prime examples – during which some 350,000 books and magazines were destroyed on magistrates' instructions: a true story less notorious but no less remarkable than the controversy surrounding *Lady Chatterley's Lover*.

The Trials of Hank Janson also details the full publishing history of the Janson stories, from 1946 right up to the present day with Telos's reissue series.

'An intriguing history of a long-gone literary genre and the downfall of a bestselling author.' Sue Baker, *Publishing News* 'Highly Recommended'

'An immensely readable book, fleshing out the story of Frances and his creation with the sort of background minutiae that bibliophiles adore, plus copious footnotes and appendices.'
Book and Magazine Collector

344pp. A5 paperback original.

Illustrated with a 16pp full colour section of many original Hank Janson book jackets.

ISBN 1-903889-84-7 (pb)
£12.99 UK $17.95 US $24.95 CAN

Some Look Better Dead

Hank Janson

A seemingly innocuous visit to a fashion show leads *Chicago Chronicle*'s ace reporter Hank Janson into a web of murder and intrigue with dark secrets from the past.

112pp. A5 paperback reprint.
Includes an introduction by
pulp historian and writer Steve Holland

ISBN 1-903889-82-0 (pb) £9.99 UK $9.95 US $14.95 CAN

Skirts Bring Me Sorrow

Hank Janson

Murder, blackmail, a femme fatale and switched identities ... just everyday problems for Hank Janson.

The Telos edition reinstates the previously-unpublished original cover artwork by Reginald Heade, which was censored when the novel first appeared in 1951.

144pp. A5 paperback reprint.
Includes an introduction by
pulp historian and writer Steve Holland

ISBN 1-903889-83-9 (pb) £9.99 UK $9.95 US $14.95 CAN

TORMENT
Hank Janson

Chicago Chronicle reporter Hank Janson is caught up in a convoluted web of intrigue involving telepathy, murder, grave robbing, pornographic photographs, infidelity and suicide! He is faced with having to uncover the links that bind all these disparate and seemingly unconnected events together and discover what really lies behind them.

Telos' publication of *Torment* marked the 50th anniversary of the book.

144pp. A5 paperback reprint.
Includes an introduction by
pulp historian and writer Steve Holland
ISBN 1-903889-80-4 (pb) £9.99 UK $9.95 US $14.95 CAN

Women Hate Till Death

Hank Janson

At a promotional event for a revolutionary new car, Hank Janson encounters cousins Doris and Marion Langham, whose wartime experiences in a Nazi concentration camp haunt them still. When a subsequent journalistic assignment leads Hank to investigate the gruesome shooting of Joe Sparman, who worked for the experimental car's manufacturer, he starts to suspect that the harrowing events of the past are having even more tangible consequences in the present ...

144pp. A5 paperback reprint.
Includes an introduction by
pulp historian and writer Steve Holland
ISBN 1-903889-81-2 (pb) £9.99 UK $9.95 US $14.95 CAN

When Dames Get Tough

Hank Janson

This anthology of ultra-rarities reprints the first three Hank Janson novellas – *When Dames Get Tough*, *Scarred Faces* and *Kitty Takes The Rap* – which initially appeared in 1946 over two volumes (with the latter two collected together under the *Scarred Faces* title). Literally only a handful of copies of the original editions now survive. Also included in this Telos anthology, as a bonus, are two Hank Janson short stories from the scarce *Underworld* magazine.

224pp. A5 paperback reprint.
Includes an introduction by
pulp historian and writer Steve Holland

ISBN 1-903889-85-5 (pb) £9.99 UK $9.95 US $14.95 CAN

ACCUSED

Hank Janson

Telos Publishing is proud to bring back into print, after more than fifty years' absence, what most fans agree is one of the very best of the classic era Hank Janson novels. *Accused* was the most heavily scrutinised book of all in the infamous Hank Janson obscenity trials at the Old Bailey in the mid-1950s, and as a result was effectively banned from British bookshops. Now readers can judge for themselves whether or not this absorbing tale of sadistic cruelty, illicit passion and violent murder really was obscene! As usual, this Telos Publishing reissue comes unedited, and complete with legendary illustrator Reginald Heade's wonderful original artwork cover.

152pp. A5 paperback reprint.
Includes an introduction by
pulp historian and writer Steve Holland
ISBN 1-903889-86-3 (pb) £9.99 UK $9.95 US $12.95 CAN

Frails Can Be So Tough

Hank Janson

Lee Shelton is a man with a tragic past and a deeply troubled present. Framed for a murder he didn't commit, forced to kidnap and chain up a beautiful passer-by – who turns out to be a millionairess – in order to avoid capture, and with a broken hypodermic needle buried in his festering arm, he finds events conspiring against him. Will he be able to get out from under all these problems, or is a lengthy prison sentence – or even death – what fate has in store for him? This intriguing thriller is the latest in Telos Publishing's acclaimed Hank Janson reissue series, and reinstates Reginald Heade's striking, previously-unpublished original artwork cover, which was censored when the book first appeared in 1951 in an attempt to avoid prosecution for obscenity.

174pp. A5 paperback reprint.
Includes an introduction by
pulp historian and writer Steve Holland
ISBN 1-903889-88-X (pb) £9.99 UK $9.95 US $12.95 CAN

KILLER

Hank Janson

Hank Janson's chance meeting with a beautiful female hitchhiker, Cora Tanter, is just the start of a thrilling tale involving an elderly archaeologist, his rich but suicidal young wife, and a haul of valuable Roman artefacts. And just who is the mysterious figure making repeated attempts to assassinate Hank himself? Add to this the complications of his on-off relationship with *Chicago Chronicle* colleague Sheila Lang, and Hank really has his work cut out this time! This reissue from Telos Publishing, complete with Reginald Heade's stunning original cover artwork, brings back into print, for the first time in decades, one of the books that featured heavily in the infamous Hank Janson obscenity trials of the 1950s.

152pp. A5 paperback reprint.
Includes an introduction by
pulp historian and writer Steve Holland
ISBN 1-903889-87-1 (pb) £9.99 UK $9.95 US $12.95 CAN